AFTERGLOW

AFTERGLOW

CLIMATE FICTION FOR FUTURE ANCESTORS

EDITED BY GRIST

NEW YORK
LONDON

Requests for permission to reproduce selections from this book should be made through our website: https://thenewpress.com/contact.

Published in the United States by The New Press, New York, 2023
Distributed by Two Rivers Distribution

ISBN 978-1-62097-758-3 (pb)
ISBN 978-1-62097-770-5 (ebook)
CIP data is available

The New Press publishes books that promote and enrich public discussion and understanding of the issues vital to our democracy and to a more equitable world. These books are made possible by the enthusiasm of our readers; the support of a committed group of donors, large and small; the collaboration of our many partners in the independent media and the not-for-profit sector; booksellers, who often hand-sell New Press books; librarians; and above all by our authors.

www.thenewpress.com

Book design and composition by Bookbright Media
This book was set in Janson Text and Refrigerator Deluxe

Printed in the United States of America

CONTENTS

Foreword by adrienne maree brown   vii

Editor's Note   xv

AFTERGLOW   1
Lindsey Brodeck

THE CLOUD WEAVER'S SONG   19
Saul Tanpepper

TIDINGS   37
Rich Larson

A WORM TO THE WISE   53
Marissa Lingen

A SÉANCE IN THE ANTHROPOCENE   71
Abigail Larkin

THE TREE IN THE BACK YARD   93
Michelle Yoon

WHEN IT'S TIME TO HARVEST   109
Renan Bernardo

BROKEN FROM THE COLONY   129
Ada M. Patterson

THE CASE OF THE TURNED TIDE   147
Savitri Putu Horrigan

EL, THE PLASTOTROPHS, AND ME   165
Tehnuka

CANVAS—WAX—MOON   185
Ailbhe Pascal

THE SECRETS OF THE LAST GREENLAND SHARK   205
Mike McClelland

Acknowledgments   225

Contributor Biographies   227

FOREWORD

WRITING FICTION ALLOWS US TO DREAM ALOUD, TO DREAM ONTO pages that we hope others will read, and to craft worlds we hope others will visit.

We are already dreaming beyond this current moment, these crises, these norms. Dreams are the foundation for what we attempt to turn into reality. Democracy was a dream (and some might argue it still is in most places, even for those who claim to be practicing it); the abolition of slavery was a dream (and some should argue it still is, while the prison industrial complex thrives); every garden we find nourishing was first a dream. The structures of our society emerged from someone dreaming it thus, for better and for worse—supremacy was dreamt up from insecure minds, racism was dreamt up from a fear of difference.

When we know things need to change, dreaming together is

one of the places we can start. I have been blessed to experience many kinds of collective dreaming, both as a movement worker and as a fiction writer. My movement work was primarily facilitation, holding space and process for groups of change-makers— people who see injustice in the world and take responsibility. I have facilitated rooms full of people committed to changing the world, listening as they dreamed together a future in which everyone has access to everything they need, a future where we care about the Earth and the children of our species in equal measure and as collective points of self-care. I have held rooms in which people debated over the priorities of the future—How can we sustain human life on earth? Eradicate racism and other systems of supremacy? Return land to Indigenous stewardship?

As a fiction writer, I often return to my memories of those rooms. The heroes of my fiction are inspired by people who want to take responsibility for the future at a collective level, especially young people. I often write about communities who are experiencing at a small scale what is changing at the grandest scale in the world. I write both to uplift these stories and strategies, and to cast the spell into the world's imagination. It could be like this. We could have reparations and regain our dignity. We could relinquish our reliance on technologies of illusion and embrace who and what we are, the beauty of our brief and miraculous lives.

I am also, like many of the writers around me, obsessed with imagining futures in which humans are thriving in right relationship to the planet. I have written stories in which humans operate in much smaller units, interconnected but living in harmony with what the land can sustain. In an age of wildfires and political inflammation, I am writing a series of stories in which we find an ally in the water itself. I intentionally try to follow in the footsteps of writers who have tackled climate change head-on. Octavia E. Butler wrote us the *Parable of the Sower* and *Parable of the Talents* from directly inside the climate crisis, and then the incredible *Xenogenesis/Lilith's Brood* collection about how humans continue two hundred years after a climate apocalypse. Butler was writing us warnings. Kim Stanley Robinson is another incredible writer of climate fiction, telling stories of how humans persist despite having made the Earth inhospitable. Alexis Pauline Gumbs, Alex DiFrancesco, Rivers Solomon, Nalo Hopkinson, and others offer us visions and pathways forward with their fiction.

But what do we do if our dream space is colonized, as I believe it is?

To colonize a place and people is to settle among them and seize political control over their land, lives, labor, beliefs, and practices. Much of the world we now live in was colonized at some point, meaning the majority of humans live in a post-colonial architecture, both physical and ideological. The dominant culture in the United States, from which I write this foreword to you, is a mix-up of various colonial efforts which both collaborated and battled over territory. One of the winning ideas was capitalism, an economic system rooted in private ownership of resources and competition-based development. As long as capitalism dictates the relationship of our species to our planet, we are losing the long game, the one in which human life gets to continue on Earth.

To decolonize is to heal the colonial wound—from the land, from the culture, from the practices, from the mind. But for many people, when we begin to speak of possible solutions—like a collaborative people-centered economy, like replacing punitive culture with a culture of accountability, like centering the needs of our children in our decision-making—it feels impossible. They cannot imagine it. In many ways, the work of decolonizing the future is the work of decolonizing our imaginations.

We have to tell stories in which the protagonists are those whose stories are least often told, recentering our attention away from the elite, the celebrities, the influencers. Making money from the exploitation of Earth and labor is an old story, boring and familiar. The stories we need to hear are of those who are aware of their conditions, attentive to what is changing in the world around us, and finding compelling paths forward. We have to literally rewire our brains to be interested in our creation and continuation, more than our destruction.

In my writing, I look for the least likely hero, and I follow their humanity, their impulse to live, their creativity in the face of challenges. I want to show how good a slow and connected future could feel. I am working to write stories where everything is not urgent, but where the pace of small pleasures and rooting into place dictate the pace of action.

I am working to decolonize my mind by writing stories that

reach back through my own lost lineage, to listen for my original instructions. I am writing stories in which the Indigenous and Black and brown people win not through domination, but through protecting what is sacred, and surviving all the way through to pleasure.

The Imagine 2200 climate-fiction contest, from Fix, Grist's solutions lab, invited writers from all over the world and across genres to participate in this exercise together. The stories in this collection are a variety of attempts to decolonize our thinking of the future, particularly on this planet, and to show what hope and utopia look like through lenses beyond our own.

Reading through the twelve stories published here allows us to dream about future climate conditions together, seeding ideas into each other's dream spaces; to realize where our dreams are overlapping and learn where our imaginations have been constrained by our realities. The writers have so many origin stories themselves, covering all manner of place, race, gender, ability, and life experience.

As one of the fortunate judges of this contest, alongside Sheree Renée Thomas, Kiese Laymon, and Morgan Jerkins, I got to open all of these portals into what people thought life on Earth could look like in 2200. Some saw us rediscovering nature, some saw us adapting to live underwater, and some saw a future beyond humanity. Every story has beauty in it—in our imaginations the future is beautiful and there is always a new horizon.

"Broken from the Colony" is a gorgeous tale in which trans

girls find acceptance and security among coral as sole survivors of a storm that submerges their Caribbean island. My notes for this story were "wow wow super wow"—we enter this mysterious, poetic flow of a story already submerged, experiencing with the protagonist an unexpected storm survival. I cannot stop thinking of this story, and the idea that the adaptations we go through to be our truest selves right here and now are actually strengthening our capacity to adapt when deeper changes unfold.

"The Cloud Weaver's Song" is a story of weaving clouds to catch water in a realm of drought, and what it might look like to imagine and act beyond that scarcity. The story feels like it has always been here—like a traditional story, a story of magic that we all need to understand. A story that already feels true even as it is fantastical in every way. I can see the world, and I can see these mythical beings who are supporting the possibility of life for their whole community. This story is also a reminder that often, the way forward is only clear to those to whom no one will listen. We have to be willing to act on what we know, take risks to unveil the path to those we love. This is one of the most beautiful direct action stories I've ever read.

In "The Secrets of the Last Greenland Shark," the last four creatures on Earth make an amazing discovery as the oldest of them finally returns home. This story will also stick with me—lately I have been really sitting in humbling meditation on the idea that the Earth will survive us, and that life will continue in some form beyond us, and that even though I feel a deep grief for what my species is up to, the future beyond us could still be curious and celebratory. This story is a gift. The ending was a deep and unexpected pleasure.

These three are just a small preview of what you are about to experience in this collection.

Read these stories slowly, give yourself time in between them to really feel the worlds that have been built in these pages. Feel the fears that sparked these imaginings, and consider the solutions. Soften into the hope, brilliance, and tenacity of these dreams.

adrienne maree brown

EDITOR'S NOTE

As the network weaver at Fix, the solutions lab at the nonprofit climate news site Grist, I spend a lot of time talking to people who are coming up with amazing solutions to the climate crisis. The job is by definition hopeful, which is great, because Fix believes that together everyone can build a cleaner, more equitable future. We write about the people and organizations doing just that.

About two years ago we started to wonder how fiction might help us bring more people into imagining that better future. I was given the great opportunity to create and lead Imagine 2200, an initiative that was as much a call to action as it was a short story contest. We wanted to connect with writers who could use their imagination to shape our climate present by envisioning our climate future. The contest drew more than 1,100 entries from eighty-five countries. Our call clearly spoke to the hearts and minds of writers worldwide.

Speculative fiction writers Tobias Buckell, Andrew Hudson, and Sarena Ulibarri spent two months reading, discussing, and debating those entries. They whittled them to twenty stories, each of which presented a unique vision of a future where we not only survive, but thrive. They handed them to our judges, adrienne maree brown, Sheree Renée Thomas, Kiese Laymon, and Morgan Jerkins, who selected three winners and nine runners-up.

The anthology you're holding collects those twelve amazing stories. In it, you'll join the last four creatures on Earth as they reminisce in their final moments. You'll visit a society that farms the skies for water. And you'll learn how a group of rebels keeps biodiversity alive. Reading this collection, you'll discover how hope and liberation mean different things to different people.

I hope that you see yourself in these stories and futures, and that you find in them ways that we, together, can co-create the abundance we deserve, and heal from violence and extraction. That's what it means to be a future ancestor.

Tory Stephens
Climate Fiction Creative Manager

AFTERGLOW

AFTERGLOW

Lindsey Brodeck

It's early summer and only a month until the last of the pods leave for the Kepler planets. Renem secured a contract for two; of course she wants me to go with her.

I need time to clear my head. She doesn't understand why, because it isn't like we'll be leaving anything behind. Our living situation is squatting on the good days and bench-sleeping on the bad. And there's no need to talk about family. Renem never knew her parents, and I buried what was left of mine years ago. We've been together for over half my life. Sometimes I wonder if it's more out of necessity than love.

I'm at Antimatter and the dance floor is packed as usual. It isn't exactly an upstanding place, but I feel at home here, like I can step out of my skin and become a part of something bigger. There's someone passing out Tangle tablets in the corner. It's gray market, probably reverse engineered. I scan it quickly—only a 0.1 percent chance of meth-mod. A good sign, but not a promise; it could still be laced with some other addictive compound. I pay the price and pop one in my mouth. As the tab dissolves, my nagging thoughts dissolve along with it. The only trace is a saccharine ache on my teeth. Soon, I am nothing but free energy mixing in with the crowd.

Usually, everyone here is so much inside their own synth-induced bliss that it's rare you'll ever get bothered. Tonight must be one of those rare occasions, because I can feel someone's eyes on me. I stop dancing and try to locate the source, but every time I strain to make sense of the shapes around me it's like I'm going the wrong way on a kaleidoscope. Blurring out of focus, everything vague and undefined. But still beautiful. There's someone running toward me, doubling back, cutting out large loops and spirals. The movement makes my head spin. I see a flash of wings as thin as cobwebs.

The crowd is shifting and feverish and I lose the jumble of colors as quickly as I first found it. If only the rainbow strobe would shut off, just for a minute. I slump down to the sticky floor, burying my face in my hands. I rub my eyes open and they sting from the sweat. But I notice something promising, something on the concrete. It is bright and yellow, glowing. It looks like a trail.

Following a near-invisible line through a packed dance floor is no small feat, especially when you're on nothing but hands and bare knees and a mid-grade party drug. By the time I'm outside,

I've had more drinks spilled on me than a champagne girl in one of those awful gentleman orgs. Need to stop thinking about that before I get even more nauseous. My vision is cutting out and soon my memory will go along with it. But not before I see it.

I'm up on the rooftop and the line is hardly linear; it's more like a maze of unspooled thread. Eventually it makes its way up a half-broken brick wall, circling a tall mural that must span over twenty feet. I don't know what I am expecting, but it isn't this.

Long wings, bubbling eyes, a body that glows green in the moonlight. It's the most beautiful insect I've ever seen. I move closer, reaching out to make contact. I trace what I can with my fingertips and take in a deep breath. It isn't paint that forms the image but something heady: laced with decay, multi-textured, alive. My optic mod explodes with names right before my vision goes. The words are all that's left imprinted on my eyelids: *Xanthoria parietina*, *Lichina pygmaea*, *Hypnum cupressiforme*.

"I saw something amazing tonight."

I'm back with Renem somehow, in our half-roofed abandoned building. She's holding me, stroking my hair. But I know she's angry. I'm shaking in her arms.

"It's always easy to find you, at least."

Animosity underneath those eight easy words. She doesn't consider that sometimes I don't want to be found. And she won't ever consider it, not if she wants to keep her savior complex going.

I try to keep the upcoming fight at bay, pleading to her that this time it was different. "There was someone who sent a message to me," I say.

She turns away. Her dark, strong face is framed by moonlight streaming in through the gaps.

"Stop acting like a child, Talli." Renem spits out my name like it's a curse. "When are you going to grow up?" At this she lets go and stands up, her warmth escaping with her.

My conciliatory efforts evaporate along with the heat. "Oh, so it's the adult choice to be slaves on 452b?" I retort. I shiver as the sweat saturating my dress turns cold. "You know we'll never make the debt up. They designed it that way."

She shakes her head, as if the point I'm making isn't one that matters at all. "You've seen the pictures. Those planets are our only hope. I could make a life for us."

She comes back to me then, trying to get under the pile of blankets. I pull away. The night is warm enough without her.

I'm seeing bees everywhere: ads in my feed—useless things like costumed clothing and jewelry and products I could never afford—and people on the street adorned with antennae and shimmery wings. I see real bees too, landing on scrawny little plants growing through the concrete and buzzing around the flowering vines that move like snakes around the downtown ruins. Maybe they've always been there, but it's the first time I'm really noticing them. I keep my optic mod on constantly so I can identify and log each new species. My favorites are the small, mostly black insects I've always assumed were flies. Now they are bees and have beautiful names: *Ceratina acantha, Hylaeus annulatus, Chelostoma philadelphi, Lasioglossum imitatum, Sphecodes monilicornis.* I can tell them apart even with the mod switched off; yellow slits near the eyes are a trademark of *Hylaeus,* and *Sphecodes'* bright red abdomen is instantly identifiable. There is something in my head too, a faint but unshakable hum. It reminds me of what a hot, lazy summer should sound like. Whenever I bring up any of this with Renem, she says I'm wasting both of our time.

It's becoming easier to distinguish the real from the fake—separating the trendy insect body mods from the type of figure I saw weeks ago. And I'm noticing something surprising inside me, a feeling I wouldn't expect myself to feel. As more of the rich leave for virgin planets and the afterglow of their ships leave me with green-yellow retinal burns, I'm not filled with worry or despair. If anything, I'm hopeful.

I'm in downtown Brexton-Maine when I spot one of them. Even with my sober mind, it's still hard to fully describe what I see. Maybe the person has some type of field scatterer on them, making them harder to track. But it's one of them. I know it; I feel it, and when I look down, there's that same wandering fluorescent yellow line.

I lose the figure quickly but I continue following the line. It leads me to a warehouse about ten blocks from where Renem and I are currently staying. I should have been spending my time scavenging in the outer zone landfills and selling what I could. At least, that's what Renem would want me to do.

I'm not scared to go inside. But when I push open those heavy metal doors, I am surprised at what I hear and see: an incessant, relentless droning, thousands of seedlings, and a single person dressed in white. A beekeeper's uniform.

"I take it you followed our trail?"

I say something to respond, but the words come out jumbled. The roar encases me, maddening and sweet, and the bright white of the fluorescent lights gives the warehouse a supernatural glow.

"More and more people are finding us." The veil hood comes off, revealing dark eyes and a tumble of long brown hair. "I'm Wyl. They/them." Their cheeks are red-flushed and shining. "What's your name?"

"Talli," I say. "She/hers."

"Welcome, Talli. The rest of those who found us today are upstairs."

Their words give me a twinge of unexpected sadness. My reaction must be obvious, because Wyl gives me a wry smile and a raised eyebrow, as if to say, "What, you thought you were the only one?" Somehow I hadn't expected others to have found this place. The mural at Antimatter, the figure in the street, it all seemed like it was designed just for me. My own map to something, a map that could save me. Save us, I mean.

As I follow them to the back of the warehouse, weaving through rows of wildly varying plant starts, I locate the source of the hum. Large beehives, which isn't surprising, but also structures that I can't quite name: huge stacks of hollowed-out wooden tubes and tracts of soil in tanks that stretch half the width of the entire wall.

"Only a few bee species live in hives, you know," Wyl says.

We walk up the industrial staircase, eventually surpassing the level of the ceiling lights. Above us is a steel trapdoor. They release the latch and push. And then there is blinding sunlight, dozens of people, and rows upon rows of flowers, vegetables, and berry bushes, and fruit trees filled with jays and chickadees.

"The world is in a lot better place than they would have us believe," Wyl says. "Yes, there is destruction, but there is also cause for hope. So much hope."

Wyl doesn't need to clarify the "they" they are speaking of. It's clear they're talking about StarSpace.

The group is a diverse one: a wave of colors and expressions that come together to form a single, composed image. I turn to face Wyl, but they have already woven their way into the center of the crowd.

"For those of you just arriving, welcome." Wyl pauses for a moment, and smiles warmly at us. "The Keepers' mission is simple. We are a group of people who have recognized a way of being that has been present on Earth for thousands of years. A way of being that centers community and kin-making with all animate beings. It is also a way that has been recognized by other people, on other planets. Tell me—" They pause, and gesture to a young man in the front of the crowd. "What pronoun would you use to describe what you see here?" Wyl points to a bee meandering lazily through the air. Unconsciously, I move closer. The insect lands on a purple sunflower—*Echinacea purpurea*—right next to me. The bee is no honeybee; the metallic green of its head and thorax makes that abundantly clear. I know the name to give it: *Agapostemon virescens.*

The man smiles in a self-conscious way, like he is afraid of being tricked. His flushed cheeks are almost as red as his shirt. "*It's* on a flower?"

Wyl smiles, but shakes their head. "That is what I assumed you would say, but we're here to show you a different way of seeing the world, and the inhabitants we share the world with. Our mission is more than beekeeping, gardening, and rewilding. We're fighting for a semantic shift too. What do any of you know about 452b, the first planet the pods landed on all those years ago?"

I'm never one to speak up in crowds, but something compels me to answer.

"The plant people living there, they can hardly tell anything apart," I say. "Not just from each other, but from anything that is alive. Everything is connected. That's why their language is so hard to understand."

Wyl nods, and I assume I've given the right answer.

"You're close, but that isn't quite it."

I stay silent. My cheeks are now flushed too.

"You are correct about one thing. The Heliogen language is certainly difficult to translate into our own. English speakers inherited a language of imperialists, one that objectifies and capitalizes on virtually everything *it* comes into contact with. The language of the Heliogens is far different. Their language emphasizes the connections between us, not the arbitrary boundaries intended to separate us. Heliogens even have a pronoun for everyone, and everything. And that pronoun is *se*. A Heliogen would never say, '*It* is flying through the air,' because they recognize the similarities we share with other animate beings as being far more important than our differences. *Se* is the ultimate form of respect, expressing the connection we—or should I say 'se'—share with all others. This bee, se pollinates our flowers; the flowers, se give us nourishment and beauty. Our words are just as important as our actions. They shape our mind, our way of seeing, our sense-making."

It is beautiful, what Wyl is saying, but also difficult to grasp. As I try to think about the way the language I speak influences the way I understand the world, I feel my thoughts go fuzzy.

"We can even use *se* to describe ourselves, for it is incorrect to think of 'you' or 'me' as composed of only human-ness. In fact, se are working together with trillions of prokaryotic cells. So this makes us amalgamations, holobionts, chimeras, constantly changing, yet one."

Wyl pauses for a moment to catch their breath. I realize I have been holding mine.

"And finally, there is another way of seeing that we find equally important, a way of seeing that recognizes change and connection as the constant. Think of the Passamaquoddy people—my people—who are indigenous to the very ground we stand on. We have a multitude of words for 'river,' 'field,' and 'wind,' among many others; words that are both animate nouns and verbs. Think of a river. How strange it is that English has only one word to describe a force that is constantly in flux. The Passamaquoddy, by contrast, have distinct words to describe where the river widens out, *kskopeke*; where se comes back in, *ksepiqe*; where se divides or comes back together, *niktuwicuwon*—just to name a few. It is difficult to change the relationship you have with your language, but it is not impossible. First, it takes awareness."

Wyl keeps giving more examples, like how classifying a field as a thing, as an "it," makes it that much easier for the land to be exploited and disrespected. Instead, if we think of a field as part of something connected and important, as an expression of the land at a point in time—*pomskute*, a field goes along—we will tend to it—to *se*—all the more justly.

"Everything shifts once you realize that it is our responsibility to take care of our home, if there is to be any hope for se to, in turn, take care of us," Wyl says. "Nature is resilient, ever-changing, adaptable. And our role as steward, as changer, is nothing new. Humans have been changing nature for tens of thousands of years. As far as geological time goes, it is only recently that this change has turned disastrous and destructive."

From radical rewilding to inner-city gardening, Wyl explains the Keepers' vision as one that includes a multitude of solutions. I look around: rich soil, large trees, an abundance of food and flowers. The scene is nothing like the sterile monocrops I'm used to seeing advertised by FarmCo. Se is half-wild and beautiful, tended by humans and thriving on top of concrete.

It has only felt like a few minutes since I arrived, but the setting sun tells otherwise. Wyl has finished talking, and I find myself sitting next to them, watching the empty clouds fill with color. I ask them how long they've been with the Keepers.

"A few years now." Wyl smiles and shades their eyes. "I can hardly remember what my life was like before them."

"If what you were saying is true, if there are thousands of you . . ."

"Then why haven't you ever seen us?"

I nod.

"You have. You just didn't know it." They stop for a moment and pick a flower from a nearby bed. *Gaillardia aristata.* "That's the problem with how people think about us. Like we must all be wearing homemade clothes and living in communes or something. Of course, some of us are that way." They laugh and twirl the flower between their thumb and forefinger. The petals are yellow-bordered and red like the sky's fading streaks. "But the point is, anyone can become a Keeper, if they want to."

"I want to." My voice comes out as a whisper.

Wyl doesn't say anything at first, but the silence isn't uncomfortable. After a few moments, they answer.

"I was hoping you'd say that. You seem right for us, Talli. And you've already become quite the citizen scientist."

I look at them quizzically. They laugh. "Don't worry, we're not tracking you. The logs you post are public, that's all."

I smile, feeling my body relax back to where it had been. At this moment, I convince myself everything will be okay. That Renem and I will be okay, and that I can make her see how much this place makes sense for us. That Earth is not a doomed planet. That there is so much possibility and potential right here.

It's too much to think about, so I try to shift back into the present. I ask Wyl if they've ever been outside of Brexton-Maine. Their laugh is small and intimate.

"Where haven't I been?" They pause for a moment before continuing. "I first started with them in New Texas, with all the Pleistocene rewilding that went on there."

I feel my jaw drop. "I heard about that. You dropped off giant tortoises and camels in the desert. Carnivores, too. Lions, cheetahs. The leaders there were furious."

"They were." Wyl grins. "It worked beautifully. We bought thousands of acres of unused, forgotten land. Of course, not fencing off that land made a few people angry. But it was worth it. We started with a few hundred animals, all from critically endangered species. Now se are thriving, and the land is more life-giving than se has been for thousands of years."

Wyl trails off. Their hair is softly blowing, and backlit by the remains of the sunset.

"You know, we've done some rewilding at a smaller scale close by," they say. "Do you want to see it?"

I can't find words strong enough to express my eagerness, so all I do is nod my head yes.

They lead me out of the building, to their car parked on the street behind it. "I haven't been in one of these in ages," I say.

Wyl grins again. "They're a lot cheaper when you don't have to pay for electricity through the city."

We drive. After half an hour, we've made it to the swampy part of the city, where flooding is the norm and anyone unlucky enough to still be living here is used to their homes being full of mold and rot. They pull off abruptly. The huge, abandoned lot doesn't seem like an important place. It is marshy, overgrown, and filled with mosquitoes. But Wyl gets out of the car anyway and I follow, treading through muck and reeds until we get to a medium-sized pond. They had said this rewilding would be at a smaller scale, but I wasn't expecting something this small, this insignificant.

"Is this it?" I ask, trying to keep the disappointment out of my voice.

"Nightfall is almost here. Be patient." They crouch and beckon me to follow suit.

Wyl was right; the sky is soon devoid of color and the heat of the day escapes into the air. At least some of the mosquitos escape with it. My back aches, and I scratch the swelling welts on my legs and arms. I am in the midst of making up some excuse when I hear something. It is vaguely human and squawky, a throaty, almost musical sound.

"We've brought life back into hundreds of places like this. *Puspahkomike*, wetlands. Have you spotted one yet?"

I shake my head, even though they probably can't see me in the dark. I feel embarrassed to ask it, but I go ahead anyway. "What is that noise?"

Wyl's voice is little more than a whisper. "Frogs, Talli. Hundreds and hundreds of frogs."

"It can't be," I whisper back. "Haven't they been extinct here for decades?" I know I'm right; I read a few years back about a fungus spreading throughout most of the Northeast, one that killed off frogs, salamanders, and other amphibians.

"At one point, yes. But there were some species that weren't susceptible to the chytrid. And we brought se here."

I keep my mouth shut, but in my head I wonder what's so great about bringing a few frogs back. The Pleistocene rewilding, that I can understand. But this, it seems like a lot of effort for nothing at all.

"Frogs are a keystone species, you know," Wyl says as if reading my mind. "Just like the megafauna we introduced in the Southwest. Ever since bringing se here, other animals have come back too. Snakes, birds, small mammals. This little pond is a fully functioning ecosystem."

My eyes aren't the only things adjusting. I peer closely at a collection of wet, shiny rocks; of course, they aren't rocks, but round, gleaming, beautiful frogs.

* * *

We are back in the car, and I want to stay in this moment forever. I force time to slow down, to notice everything surrounding me. The way Wyl's nose curls up ever so slightly, the smattering of freckles across their face. Their deep brown eyes that look just like Renem's. Renem. Wyl is playing some type of sad, sweet music that helps stretch out the time. It is wordless, classical-sounding. But someone like me wouldn't know. It seems like Wyl is driving slower than they have to, maybe they feel the gravity of the situation too. I'm suspended on one endpoint of a pendulum's arc, and I'm not sure if I'll ever be able to swing back. My real life isn't rewilding and honoring the world with new words; it is tense conversations, struggling to survive, and convincing Renem we don't have to leave Earth.

Wyl breaks the silence. "Can you spare a few more hours?" they ask. "I need to show you one more thing."

We're already in my part of the city, only a few minutes away from the long-abandoned butcher shop Renem and I are currently calling home. It's been hours since I last contacted her.

"If you have to go back, I understand." Wyl stops the car and taps their fingers nervously on the dashboard.

"A few hours won't hurt," I say.

Wyl smiles and pulls a U-turn. "It'll be worth it. I promise."

Those few hours pass quickly. We—well, mostly Wyl—talk about everything from the flawed rhetoric of twentieth-century environmentalists—"Their intentions were good, but why was 'Save the Earth' their motto? Why didn't they just say 'Save ourselves'?"—to the Keepers' terraforming projects in Siberia, the Sahara, and along the Gulf of Mexico. Their chatting makes time snap back into a more natural pace, but it still isn't fast enough for me to forget about the growing knot in my stomach.

As if on cue, I receive a message from Renem: *Where are you?*

Even though there isn't any audio accompanying the neuro-text, I know her tone is sharp and accusatory. I also know that she is probably worried. I ignore it for close to half an hour, but eventually reply: *I'm trying to figure out something for us.*

Her response is hardly a surprise. *You're crazy if you think that cult can save you.*

It could save us, I reply.

We're leaving tomorrow.

The sky cracks and goes red. I cower in the passenger seat and cover my ears. Another swarm of shiplets breaking through the atmosphere. The crimson streak soon fades into blackness. I had forgotten that it's tomorrow. The pang in my stomach intensifies.

"We're almost there," Wyl says.

We're out in the open countryside, or what has been turned into countryside. The bones of some now-useless industrial com-pound stick out of the rolling grasses and flowers, its strangeness amplified by the full moon. The road curves sharply. It's difficult to see it all clearly, but as we pass around a large hill, dozens of small houses, rows of half-wild gardens, and glinting solar panels come into stark relief.

"I thought you'd like to see one of our communities." Wyl steps out of the car and gestures for me to follow. We walk to one of the garden plots; the intertwined pea and squash tendrils snake around the trellis and appear alien in the moonlight.

Wyl plunges their hand into a bag tied around the trellis and pulls out a gleaming handful. "Seeds can be planted anywhere. They don't need perfect conditions to grow." They drop several into my outstretched palm and close my fingers around se tightly. "Nature never went away in our city. I know you know this. Se just needs tending—stewardship. Will you be one of our Keepers?"

As I'm about to reply, I hear the ping of another message. Tears spring to my eyes, tears equally composed of mourning and relief. The drops land wet and alive and seep into the soil below me. I take my gaze upward, away from the seeds in my hand and eye-to-eye with Wyl. And I nod.

THE CLOUD WEAVER'S SONG

Saul Tanpepper

"YOUR GREAT-GRAND-*ABO* TEN TIMES REMOVED WAS THE LAST OF the Danakil Afar," I say, settling back against the cushion. "And the first to construct the towers."

A breeze passes in through the open door and dries the sweat on our brows. Tonight is the first time the temperature has been cool enough to leave the windows open, and the rooms fill with the humid aroma of the day's harvest.

"Before the Great Drying swept across the land, the Afar were a nomadic people of the Horn, shepherds mainly, who kept to themselves. Afterward, they became builders and salt traders. Your great-grand-*ahde* ten times removed came from the highlands."

Senait fidgets. Matters of ancient history hold little interest for her. She asks to hear about the Cloud Weavers instead.

"Let your *ahde* finish, little one," *abo* Limi gently chides. "It is important that you know where you come from."

But I smile down at my daughter. I draw her hair away from her eyes and ask, "How do you know about them?"

"Tes told me. He says we are Sky People, and that our rightful place is with them, weaving the clouds."

"Tesfay," Limi murmurs. He rolls his eyes, but gives me an amused look.

"Your brother's head is already in the clouds," I say, chuckling. "But I will make a deal with you, Senait. I will tell you about the Weavers, if you promise to go to sleep right after I am finished."

"And also the Thief of Sand," Senait says, sitting up straighter in her bed. Her eyes sparkle mischievously, belying the exhaustion she tries so hard to hide.

Abo Limi bellows out a laugh. "Our daughter! I do not think that she wishes to sleep at all tonight!"

But I know she will slumber, and soon, for the Weavers and the Sand Thief are two parts of the same story, and it is not very long in the telling. And afterward, maybe then she will understand why her older brother's audacious claims are both right and wrong.

As for *abo* Limi, he is less anxious about our daughter's weariness than for my own work yet to come, for there is so much still to do and too few hours before the sun will next rise.

* * *

In the history of our people, there has never been a land more inhospitable than the Danakil. Even in the time before the Great Drying, in what was known as the Afar Triangle of the Great Horn, there existed a place so hot and so parched that almost nothing grew. Sulfur springs bubbled up from the ground wherever you stood, spewing poison that painted the rocks yellow and turned the sky a sickly gray. And yet, in such an inhospitable place, isolated and against all odds, a humble people thrived for a thousand years.

But the world was changing, growing hotter and drier, and soon even the hardiest of the Afar were driven away by the intolerable heat. They migrated inland, for the only other direction was the sea, and they surely could not go there. They ended up in the midlands of the Great Horn, which was a place of many different climates. In some areas, where the temperature had long been cooler and the air wetter, forests stood thick and tall. In others, the land was flat and suitable for growing crops. But it was in the dry lands there, among the towering termite mounds and the scorpions, that the solitary Afar found familiar surroundings. So that is where they settled, even though it was not their home, for I think you will agree that it is always better to take shelter in a stranger's house than to refuse to leave your own when it is burning to the ground.

At the same time, the people of the milder midland climes, farmers mostly, were being forced deeper into the interior by the heat. There was once a beautiful city called Asmara, high on the

Kebessa Plateau, a mile and a half into the sky. Asmara was a wondrous place, where for 100,000 years the clouds drenched the air each night and rains nourished the soil. The rivers that flowed down its escarpments fed the lowlands and eventually emptied into the sea.

The ancient name Asmara comes from the phrase *arbate asmera*, which in the original Tigrinya means "the four women who made them unite." Many centuries before, this land had been under constant threat from a common enemy. Now, as before, it was the women who brought the clans together to defend against this new danger. For a while, Asmara became a sanctuary to anyone seeking refuge from the Great Drying.

But the heat and drought were unrelenting foes, and they drove more and more people to the city on the plateau. Week after week they came. Year after year. And because there was only so much land to hold them all, war became inevitable.

For a hundred years, the fighting waged.

Now, just as there is no amount of conflict, no matter how bitterly fought, which can alter the course of nature, no volume of human blood could quench the thirst of the Great Drying. The deserts continued to expand, spreading until they reached the very ankles of the beloved city on the plateau.

It is said that necessity makes us do what we must in order to survive. Eventually, the rains began to evaporate before ever reaching the ground, and the rivers dried long before spilling into the sea. So, the women of Asmara rose again and taught themselves how to harvest the nightly mists with threads spun from molten glass. For a while, it helped.

But the thirst of the Great Drying was like that of the hyena's: never slaked. Not satisfied with stealing the fog from all the lands beneath Asmara's feet, it reached up and took them from her, too.

Once more, necessity made the people do what they must in order to survive. The peaceful Afar had long since retreated into the clouds by building towers that reached even higher than the Kebessa Plateau. Now it was their brothers' and sisters' houses burning to the ground. And so they welcomed them all into the sky, where the mists were still plentiful and ripe for harvesting.

Semhar Ibrahim was a weaver of webs. Each night, she assumed the skin of a spider and set out from her little hole to spin her delicate threads. High above the ground, where the clouds formed, she carefully laid out line after endless line, each as thin as a hair and as long as a mile. To harvest the dew that condensed upon them, she gently plucked each string, sending them vibrating along their entire length. Each wire carried its own unique note, and when played together they sang the song of the Weavers. As the droplets traveled down the wires, they merged and grew fat, creating a delicate river suspended in the sky. This is how the people harvested the clouds so that all might live. And each night, when you heard the tune, you would know how heavily laden the wires were with mist, depending on how melodious or melancholic the notes sounded.

Semhar was still a young woman when her dear friend, Alimirah Kadafo, fell to Earth.

Ali, as he was known by her, was an orphan. His mother and father had died when he was still but a child no taller than a grown man's hip. He knew only of his parents' trade from the faintest memories and of the stories others told him. But as soon as he was old enough, he donned the skin of the termite, just as his *abde* and *abo* had, and also as their forebears had done before them, all the way back to when they first raised their homes into the sky. Only the descendants of the Afar were allowed to wear the termite skins, for no one else dared to erect the towers so high, where the air was so thin. And no others could make the long and treacherous descent each day to where the air was oven hot and desert dry, to collect the sand they needed to build their houses and to harvest the salt the people needed to survive.

For months, Semhar had been weaving longer into the night than she was supposed to, constructing larger and more intricate webs in order to better capture the dwindling mists. The air had been growing drier, which the leaders said was due to the yearly shift in seasons. But she felt in her bones that this time was different. The capricious clouds seemed less willing than ever to relinquish their bounty to her web. Yet for all her worrying, the leaders of the Council did not seem very concerned.

One morning, several weeks before Ali's fall, as Semhar made her way back home, she encountered him preparing for his daily descent to the ground. Usually, she would only see him in the evenings, after he had already made his rounds trading with the growers for food and the weavers for water. The two young friends would sit together and eat their supper, watching the sun drop onto the barren Kebessa Plateau far to the west. The darkness would settle in and the mists would rise toward their backs. And when the fog overtook them and blanketed the stars above, he would go off to bed, whilst she would don her spider skin and begin to spin her web.

Seeing him that morning, she realized just how late she was in returning. He warned her to be more careful, for the rising sun would melt her threads, and she could fall. He did not wish for her a fate similar to the one his parents had suffered years before.

As she watched him descend into the morning mist below, she had a thought: *Tonight, I will spin my web down there, for that is where the clouds have gone.*

But her parents told her no. "It is too dangerous," they said. "It is too hot and the winds are too unpredictable. And besides, how can we collect the water if the webs are below the cisterns? You must continue to weave the clouds as we have done for generations: high above us."

"But the clouds are thicker below."

"Above us, Semhar," they repeated. "Each year, the Great Drying chases the clouds higher and higher. It has been this way for two hundred years. And it is why we must build our towers a little taller each day."

Semhar was defiant. She knew the clouds were no longer rising. In fact, they were falling.

"This is a temporary change," they assured her. "We are Sky People, Builders of Towers and Weavers of Clouds."

"But we were not always so," Semhar countered.

"Our dearest *wulad*, listen to your parents. Do not look below for answers, for you will not find them. Our ancestors have taught us this valuable lesson."

But the ancestors had also taught that necessity made them do what they must in order to survive. Semhar believed the Sky People's very existence, like that of their forebears, lay once more in the balance.

"The clouds are shifting," she told Ali when she met him for supper that evening. "They are no longer as high as they used to be."

Ali ate his injera thoughtfully, but did not reply. His was a simple life of climbing and gathering and climbing and bartering, day after day. He did not like to think about change. Change was what had happened when his *abo* and *ahde* died. In fact, he disliked it so much that his first instinct was to refuse to acknowledge it at all. But Semhar was his dear friend, and he loved and respected her, for she had a keen mind and always spoke the truth. Also, he too had sensed the shift in weather, and it was not the same seasonal cycle he had witnessed in years past. Each morning, the mists wet the tower bases longer and lower, and it took him extra time to make the treacherous climb to the ground. More than once, he had nearly slipped and fallen.

"Today," she told him, "I will need an extra allotment of sand."

"I have already given you all I can spare," he replied. "How much more can you weave?"

"I wish to spin a whole extra web."

"You already use up every minute of darkness on the one."

"But I haven't used up all the mist."

"Semhar, if I let you have more, the builders will begin to notice the deficit."

"Tomorrow morning," she pressed, as if she hadn't heard a single word he said, "I will build a second web. This one will be lower, while the mists are still beneath us and the sun hasn't burned them away."

He scoffed. "And how will you harvest the water then? The drops will fall uncollected to the ground and be wasted. The desert does not need the rain as we do."

"I wish to prove a point to the Council. And if I am to be confident that I am right, I must first prove it to myself."

"If they find out, you will be punished for breaking the rules. The leaders are like lions, always hunting the weak to make way for the strong. They will take your skin away from you and let someone else weave the clouds instead. What will you do then?"

"There is an old saying: 'When spider webs unite, they can capture a lion.' The leaders are stubborn, this is true, but they are not stupid. I will spin my webs to capture their attention. Only then will I make them see that things are changing, even if they are changing in ways they might not want or expect them to."

"They are comfortable with their life up here in the sky."

"But we cannot keep building higher and breathing thinner air, while chasing clouds that are no longer there."

Ali considered this for a long time. As he did, Semhar turned her back to the sunset for the first time and instead watched the mists rolling in from a distant sea she had only ever seen in her dreams. Finally, when the first delicate drops of dew began to reach up and caress their skin, Ali told her what he would do.

It was a tremendous amount of extra work for him, but Ali believed in his friend. It also helped that he shared her concerns. The clouds were shifting, and if the trend continued, as Semhar believed it would, they would eventually have no more mist to harvest.

The extra thousand pounds of sand he carried threatened his skin's grip as he climbed the tower that evening. It took him far longer than usual to return to the top, and he was exhausted when he arrived.

"Why are you so late, Alimirah Kadafo?" the builders demanded. "We were worried you had fallen, just as your parents did."

"No reason," he told them.

"No reason? Are you embarrassed for falling asleep whilst gathering sand in the desert? You must be more careful, or else you will dry up like the salt."

"Will you trade for your allocation or not?"

"Why should we? You were late," they repeated. "We have already traded with someone else for tomorrow's work."

"What am I supposed to do with the sand I have today?"

"We will take it anyway, but give you nothing in return. Tomorrow, make sure you are back in time, or else we will tell the Council that you no longer deserve to wear the skin."

This will not work, Ali thought, as he left the builders. *I will just have to tell Semhar at supper that I cannot get her extra sand for her wires.*

But it was too late to see her that evening, for the sun was already beginning to set and the mists were coiling at their feet. Semhar would have finished eating by now, and Ali still had salt yet to trade for his own dinner.

He went looking for her the next day, after he had returned from the ground at the usual time with his usual load and had given the builders their sand and traded his salt away. She was flush with excitement, and barely allowed him any chance to speak while they ate.

"I have not seen so much water in a very long time," she told him. "If this continues, as I expect, then I will soon tell the leaders."

"You cannot do that." He told her what had happened the day before. "It takes me too long to gather the extra sand and far more effort to climb the tower, so that by the time I have returned, the builders have already received their allocations from the other gatherers. They still take my sand and give me nothing in exchange, so that I am left with little to show for my efforts. I am sorry, Semhar, but I have no extra sand for you this evening."

Ali lay in bed for a long time without sleeping that night. He couldn't get Semhar's disappointment from his mind. High above him, the weavers built their webs to harvest the mists, and the songs their webs sang were the saddest he had ever heard. He decided then that he would leave earlier the next morning, an extra hour before sunrise, to gather Semhar's sand. The towers would still be slick with dew, and the climb would be especially perilous, but he knew that she was right. If she was willing to break the rules for her convictions, then the risks he took were worth it.

Every morning for the next month, he rose long before dawn, donned his termite skin, and climbed down to the desert below. Every day of that month, he toiled in the baking-hot sun to gather the extra sand for his friend. And every evening, he told her where he had stashed it, so that she could spin her extra web. She did not care that the water she collected spilled unused to the ground. "I am doing this to be certain that I am right," she told him.

"I hope it will not take too long before you are," he replied.

"It won't. Soon, the lions will have no choice but to listen to reason."

"And why do you think they will?" he asked.

"Because the water in the cisterns is beginning to drop."

She was so proud of her work that he would not tell her how many times he had nearly fallen, or how the extra burden was wearing on his skin. He made his repairs as best as he could, but he knew that it was only a matter of time before it would fail.

The morning before Ali's last day on the towers dawned especially hot. After less than an hour on the ground, he was forced to begin his long ascent carrying only his usual burden of sand and none of salt. As he climbed, he told himself that Semhar would just have to do without tonight. But when he reached the place where he had been hiding her extra allotment, he decided to give it all to her. He could not bear for her to be disappointed. And what she was doing was just too important, not just to her, but to all the People of the Sky.

The builders were furious, and they threatened to tell the leaders of his indolence. Ali didn't care that they were wrong. Soon they would see what he and Semhar were doing, and they would have to acknowledge the truth. The clouds were shifting. The cisterns were drying. But most important of all, the Great Drying was drawing to an end.

Instead, they caught him the next day hiding the sand he had collected, and they took him straight to the Council.

"Alimirah Kadafo," the leaders said, "why are you stealing sand from the builders?"

"How can I steal sand that I have collected? It is mine to trade as I see fit."

"That is not how it is done. We are all essential parts of this community. Each of us plays an important role. Some grow food, some make clothes. Some harvest water, and others build. You collect sand and salt. Without these things, how can we do what is necessary to survive? When you break this chain, you steal from us all. When one of us fails, we all risk falling.

Semhar did not hear of Ali's banishment until she returned from her weaving the next morning. All night, she had suspected something terrible had happened to him, because he hadn't met her for supper, and the cache where he hid her sand had been empty. When she learned of his fate, she went straight to the Council to beg for a change of heart. But Ali was already gone, and the leaders would not be persuaded to allow him to return. "Someone stronger now wears his skin," they told her. "Someone else who is willing to do the work as it has been done for generations."

"You have made a terrible mistake!" she cried.

"Semhar Ibrahim," they scolded, "your job is to collect the water, not to worry about the sand or those who would steal it from us."

"But how can I collect the water if there are no clouds?"

"By continuing to weave. Be patient, for the mists will return. Every year, the Great Drying pushes them higher, which is why we must build our towers taller. Without sand, we cannot do that. Without water, we cannot survive."

"The cisterns are falling because there is no water to collect."

"The air is dry, this is true. But it is nothing to worry about. Soon, the seasons will shift again, and the clouds will return. Build your webs as you have been taught, and before you know it the wires will once again sing a joyous song. Then you will see that we are right. Are you not a Cloud Weaver, after all?"

"I am," she declared. "But it is also true that I am the thief of sand, not Alimirah Kadafo. I asked him to give it to me, so that I might weave an extra web each night."

The Council members glanced one to another in puzzlement. "It is not stealing, when you are using it for the betterment of the community. Your extra work is to be commended."

"The mist I gathered was never collected. I let it fall to the ground."

"How could this be?"

"Because I wove my lines below the cisterns, where the nightly mists have lately formed."

"There is nowhere for the water there to collect," they said in astonishment, for they still did not comprehend her intent. "Why would you do such a wasteful thing?"

"To prove that we must stop looking ever higher. The answer is below us. The Great Drying is over."

"We are the People of the Sky, young Semhar Ibrahim. But if you wish to forsake your birthright, then that is your decision. Tomorrow, at first light, you will be taken to join your friend on the ground."

* * *

It took her nearly the whole night to descend the tower in her stolen spider skin. The machine was not built for climbing, but for dangling and spinning. She found Ali sitting in the shadow at the base, his mouth open to capture the drops that fell from the tattered remnants of a month's worth of secret webs. It was the only thing keeping him alive.

Each night after that, she climbed to where the mists rolled in and wove a new web using the sand that he brought her to spin into glass each day. Together, they collected what water they could, although most of it fell uncaptured to the ground.

They found the first seedling a month later. And within six months, the ground beneath the towers had turned into a garden.

"She is asleep," *abo* Limi whispers.

I kiss my precious daughter on the cheek, and she doesn't even stir, for she is exhausted from her hard work. I know that when she harvests the crops each day, she looks to the skies and thinks that what we are doing here on the ground is not so exhilarating. She takes after her brother in that way. Someday, she will stay awake long enough to hear the story to its completion. Maybe it will be tomorrow, or perhaps next year. Maybe it will even be before the Sky People's cisterns empty for good, and they realize the Great Drying is finally over. Then they, too, will come down from the towers, and she will understand that this is the day for which we have been preparing. It is why I don my skin each night and weave my webs in clouds that no longer form so high in the sky. We need the rain. But so does the Earth.

"Ready, Semhar?" my dear *sebai* Alimirah asks as he finishes checking my harness.

I eagerly nod, for the mists are already forming, and they look to be especially thick tonight. "Sleep well, my children," I whisper. "And dream of the Weaver's song, for tonight the wires will sing with joy."

TIDINGS

Rich Larson

MARADI, NIGER: 2038

"It's not working," Tsayaba says. She shakes her head in disgust. "Kai!"

"Just wait," Ouma says, adjusting her scarf with shivering hands. "Yi hankali. Give it a minute."

It's a cold, dusty day—harmattan season is so unpredictable now, even with the weather drones they balloon up from Zinder and Niamey. The sky is choked gray, so full of dust that the sun is a smeary yellow blob that makes Ouma think of a lemon candy.

She takes one from her jacket pocket and hands it to Tsayaba, who stares at it. "This has a plastic wrapper, Ouma," she says. "Are you trying to drive me crazy?"

Ouma unpeels it and pops it into her own mouth instead. She

knows her older cousin is already a little—not *crazy*; Ouma has been reading e-flets on why that is a stigmatized and offensive term—but a little different. In a good way, a driven way, a furious-thrumming-brain-too-big-for-her-beautifully-braided-head way.

That is why she made money moving memes, why she went away to Nigeria to study biochem in Kano and then biotech in Lagos, why she dropped out to set up her own tiny genelab. But she never stopped messaging, and calling when she could.

And now she is back here, in dusty Maradi, where she and Ouma grew up together, to test out the little biological machine she has been tinkering with for a year and a half. Or for a whole damn century, depending on when you ask her.

The nameless thing is about the size of Ouma's clenched fist, modeled after a waxworm's digestive tract, slick-skinned and perched on cilia that should let it scuttle easily through the sand in a way jointed Bostobots still struggle with.

But the thing is not moving.

"It was perfect in all the sims," Tsayaba mutters. "In the lab tests, too. I filled my whole room with sand and trash."

She punches a few rubbery keys on her brute of a laptop, the one Ouma knows she tried to build only from old parts, to avoid unethically mined gold and tungsten, but finally had to buy new semiconductors for. Hopefully this will not be a giving-in day too.

"Lots of things don't work out here," Ouma says, bracingly. "My blockphone glitches sometimes too."

She winces after she says it, because she doesn't think block-phones and crawly genelab things work the same way, and she doesn't want Tsayaba to think she is stupid. But her older cousin is too kind to think things like that, and too distracted anyway.

"I wanted to do it here," Tsayaba mutters, rubbing her eyes. "I wanted this to be the place it starts, because it's the place *I* started. Where our family started. Where you taught me I can do important things."

Ouma feels proud of that, because she always assumed that the important things were learned in Kano and Lagos. She wants Tsayaba's thing to work, so she crouches down and presses the wrapper from her lemon candy against its membranous skin and hopes hard.

The wrapper slides through an unseen mouth and dissolves into tiny grains that swirl through the thing's rubbery body, like a little sandstorm. The thing wriggles its cilia feet. It notices the flimsy black shopping bags all around, sticking up from the street like blooming flowers, and suddenly it is hungry. It starts to move.

"It just needed to whet its appetite," Ouma says.

"I was going to try that next," Tsayaba says, but she beams. She wraps her arm around Ouma. "Thank you. And thank you for coming outside with me. I know you are freezing."

Ouma squeezes her back, imagining Tsayaba's dream: a whole swarm of the biomachines crawling through the sand, swimming through the ocean, breaking down tons upon tons of low-density polyethylene without a wisp of greenhouse gases escaping. It's a thrilling vision.

"What will you name it?" she asks. "Maciyin roba? Plastic eater?"

Tsayaba smiles without taking her eyes off the thing. "I don't know. I'll think."

PRAGUE, CZECHIA: 2044

Kat meets Jan off Lask@, one of those local splinter apps that only takes NFT payments and swears to never memorize your face and biometric data and send it straight to the Devil. The rub with going splinter is that the dating pool shrinks to a dating puddle; the un-rub is that the people splashing around in it tend to be more interesting.

Like Jan the nouveau-anarchist, who brought his own bottle of bacteria-brewed beer to the top of Letna Hill and is somehow pulling off a floral-printed suit. He offers an elbow—Prague is post-vax, but the Big One hit hard here and the greeting hung on.

"Which is for the best," Jan says. "Because the Bigger One, you know, it's around the corner."

Kat doesn't want to think about that, not tonight. She thinks about it enough during the daytime, where her job is prepping samples and lab equipment at Charles University, for the researchers working on plug-and-play mRNA to tackle whatever superbug pops up next.

She thinks about it every too-hot summer, whether she spends it here in Prague or back home in Rotterdam. Climate shift means people shift means overcrowding and deforestation and more vectors for disease and—

"Let's get drunk," Kat says, because it's been a long week.

Jan's amenable to that. They finish the bottle and refill it at the garden brewery; Kat orders in her clumsy Czech, without needing to consult her babelapp, and Jan applauds in a way that would feel sarcastic if not for his beaming smile.

Three or four bottles later, they take a walk around Holešovice. It's beautiful at night, in the blurry orange glow of the streetlamp: the old Communist-era architecture is retrofitted with solar windows and rooftop gardens, green and gray measures. The parks have all been expanded.

They wander through one with the backs of their hands not quite brushing, then Jan looks at her in a particular way and Kat really wants to kiss him right on his beer-smelling mouth, so she does it. The electricity of it makes her forget about all the incoming disasters.

Three or four minutes later, they're at Kat's apartment. The make-out starts in the cramped lift and continues into the cramped flat. She clears off the couch and then helps Jan peel his shirt off, both of them fumbly and excited, and when it clears his tousled head Kat is face-to-face with a hollow-cheeked woman in a boat.

Kat blinks. The woman blinks back. The crisp image, rendered in nano ink, is a livestream.

"Uh, Jan? Who's on your stomach?"

Jan glances down. "Oh. I forgot."

He prods his slightly beer-wobbly gut. A name appears in the nano ink: *Tharanga Mendis.*

"It is hard for me to read upside down," Jan says. "But that. She is a refugee from Negombo. The wet bulb temperature is thirty-eight now. People cannot sweat, so they leave or they die."

Kat loses her booze buzz to the old cycle: guilt, annoyance at having to feel guilt on a night where all she wanted to do was hook up, guilt for the annoyance.

"You shouldn't be skincasting people's suffering," she says sharply. "Or sharing their faces. It's gross."

Jan's slate-gray eyes turn solemn. "It's only sort of gross," he says. "Her face is already known. This is a feed from border surveillance. I'm watching them watching her, and everybody else in the boat."

Kat frowns. "Accountability?"

Jan shakes his head and grins his lopsided grin. "Better," he says. "Catalonia is only letting in migrants with proof of employment."

The smart tattoo shifts, showing a child now. They pull faces at whatever border drone is circling their vessel.

"With enough people streaming them, they can be classified as performers," Jan says. "We had a legal AI do up the contracts." He holds up his phone, and Kat sees the same feed. "I have it going everywhere," he says. "Not just the tattoo."

"If that works, it's only going to work once," Kat says, slumping down onto the couch. "You know that, right?"

"That's okay," Jan says. "We have lots of ideas. We just have to keep, you know, implementing. One little thing at a time." His forehead creases. "Did you still want to have sex?"

Kat rubs at her face. "I don't know. Kind of." She glares. "How do you *forget* you have that playing on your stomach? How can you keep things—partitioned, like that?"

"Because it's not my responsibility," Jan says. "It's everybody's responsibility. And not everybody is doing their part, but a lot of people are, and I trust those people a lot." He shrugs. "So do what you can, let go of the rest."

Kat shuts her eyes. The last thing she wanted to think about tonight was climate refugees battling draconian border security, but the world is too small, too hot, too claustrophobic, to avoid thoughts like that anymore—even for a night.

"Shirt stays on," she says, pushing it back into his chest. "But, uh, send me the stream first."

This is just how things are now. Kat does what she can, and lets go of the rest.

SITE OF IDC-59, AUSTRALIA: 2066

It's so strange to be back at the detention center, to walk along the barbed wire fence and past the somber gray tents. Eli's grandson pleaded with him not to come, because he is learning about trauma responses in school and thinks the place might trigger a panic attack Eli's old hard-thumping heart can no longer take.

But Eli wanted to come, badly. He wanted to remember. Now he leads the way toward E-Tent, where he grew up with his *abbá* and *ammá* and the ghosts they had brought with them when they fled Myanmar for their lives. He scuffs his feet in the red dirt, and remembers pretending the rippled sand was a wave-tossed sea. He fantasized about water a lot. There was never much of it in the camp.

There still isn't. The sun is blistering hot and the new refugees, splayed in the scant shade of the tents, have salt crusted around their lips. They move their mouths in the way Eli knows means their tongues are dry, bone-dry. Their faces are tired, and familiar even though he doesn't know them.

The new guards, mostly men, wear the same old dark green jackets. Eli knows that most of them are lounging inside with a fan, but the ones patrolling outside are drenched in sweat, irritable from the heat and ready to displace their annoyance at the slightest provocation.

Their heavy boots are red from the dust and black fobs hang from their belts like ticks. All the children daydreamed about stealing one of those fobs, but instead of leaving the camp, which was the entire world, they mostly wanted to get into the kitchens to find the chocolate bars one particular guard always ate right in front of them.

That was the same guard who tripped him, once, when their game of tag got too close to him. Eli remembers sprawling in the dirt and smacking his head on a piece of gravel. He remembers seeing the surprise and regret on the man's bristly face, but only for an instant, before he sealed it up with the usual scowl and told Eli to go have his cut cleaned.

Eli's *ammá* told him, later in the tent, that cruelty filters downward—like the mercury in the fish she used to study. She said the hardest thing in the world to do is absorb someone else's cruelty and not pass it along.

"How are you feeling?" little Mohib asks, squeezing his hand. "Dada?"

"It's very well done," Eli says, and pulls off his sweat-suctioned goggles.

The virtual memorial disappears, leaving only a tracery of AR guidelines in the red dirt, a few scuttling oumas hunting down traces of plastic.

The actual camps vanished more slowly, through years of policy battles fought by second-generation migrants and certain Indigenous politicians. First the offshore detention centers were dismantled, then those of the mainland, and now, at last, they exist only as a bad memory.

Eli thought it was better to forget completely. The idea of the memorial—splicing the same surveillance systems that kept so many desperate souls contained, all the footage from those miserable years—somehow seemed like moving backward.

But now that he has seen it, the forgiving without forgetting, he realizes its power to ensure that the cruelty is not passed along.

"Your heart, though," Mohib says, blinking. "How is your heart?"

Eli looks down at his grandson. For a moment, despite the crisp, clean runners and bioelectric shirt, he sees himself at the same age: scrawny, dark-eyed, still full of a restless energy. But he will never have fences around him.

"Full," Eli says. "And good."

Mohib breathes a big sigh of relief that implodes his small chest. Eli breathes too.

CYGNET COMMUNITY, DËNÉNDEH TERRITORY: 2099

Suma's idea is ridiculous, when Cade takes a step back from it, but they're fully invested now. They've both been scrounging materials for weeks, digging through every tech-tomb in walking distance of the commune, hunting down everything the printer needs to make a tweaked babeltech rig.

So when Suma comes skipping out of the solar-coated printer shack on Thursday afternoon, waving the final product in the air, Cade is chest-choked with hope and anxiety for the ending of their kid's latest dream. Suma is bright for a ten-year-old, but the blueprint was complicated as shit and she's not Tsayaba Issoufou.

"It's going to work," Suma says sternly, and Cade realizes she somehow ferreted out their doubt.

Cade considers managing expectations. "Su," they say, "I'm really, really proud of you."

Suma's brown cheeks flush, and she does the little wriggle she does to absorb excess praise.

Cade helps her set up the rig right along the garden fence, where the moose has been doing the most damage. At first the young bull was content to crane over the top and snatch gene-tweaked apples from the spindliest tree branches, but lately he prefers smashing through the metal mesh and trampling all over the rhubarb.

The commune was about to reach a unanimous vote for printing up a swarm of botflies to keep the moose away—their little electric stingers pack enough punch to deter even the occasional pizzly bear that wanders south—but Suma proposed negotiating. Which meant establishing a channel of communication.

Cade watches as Suma checks all the wireless ports and makes sure the responder is safely encased in its rubber box. Their daughter has always been fascinated by nonhuman persons: the orca colony off the coast of Old Vancouver, which used babeltech to negotiate fishing territories with the Northwest Coalition of First Nations. The roving corvid communities that sometimes fill the talknet with jumbled stories and legal disputes.

As far as Cade knows, nobody has ever successfully used babeltech to talk to a moose before. But improbable doesn't mean impossible—every time Cade looks around, they see improbable things that got done. Replacing the vast canola and wheat fields with polycultures. Dismantling the bones of the ancient oil industry, all the wells and rigs and derricks, to build wind farms and supply commune printers with raw materials.

Absorbing the countless climmigrants from flooded islands

and deadly heat, settling them across the prairies instead of the vanishing coastal cities, establishing hundreds of small villages like the one Cade and Suma call home.

So when the bull shows up the next morning, and bed-headed Suma grabs her tablet and races to the porch, Cade hopes they can add talking to a moose to the list. Their daughter links up to the babeltech. They both watch as the bull ambles up to the fence, as per usual, and starts sniffing.

He feels the static field from the babeltech, and wriggles his big, bony shoulders in a way that almost reminds Cade of their daughter.

"Hello," Suma says, voice shaking a bit from excitement. "My name is Suma."

The moose swings his big head left, then right. Snorts.

"Can you stop wrecking the fence?" Suma asks. "We could give you a bucket of apples to eat, if you like. And some spare rhubarb to step on."

The babeltech kicks in, and the synthesized representation of the moose's nonhuman person neural processes comes blaring through Suma's tablet.

"FUCK. FUCK. FUCK. FUCK."

Suma blinks in surprise. "Cade?" she says, in a low voice. "Why's he saying that?"

Cade tries to keep the laugh down, and it nearly bursts their belly. "Uh, I think it's rutting season," they say. "Maybe he'll be more conversational in a couple weeks."

Suma purses her lips. "If the moose is allowed to say it, can I say it too?"

"Just once," Cade says. "Since you got babeltech to work with a cervine. You earned it, kiddo."

Suma grins. "Even if he only cusses at us, this is still so fucking cool."

KO PHANGAN, THAILAND REPUBLIC: 2132

Nam takes her boat out in the late afternoon, when the sky is travel-holo blue and sunshine is sparkling the water. She takes 112 net-friends with her. They fill her goggle lenses with animated hearts when they see the aquamarine waves, when they feel the salt spray on her nerve suit.

She cuts against the swell; the motor hums, converting solar charge to forward motion to sheer happiness. The clear water teems with shoals of technicolor fish and the occasional ouma straining microplastics. Sometimes she still comes across mega-plastics, too: ancient Singha bottles and disposable gloves, relics of a time that sometimes feels mythical to her, that even had a king.

When her net-friends catch sight of the dolphins, their animated hearts explode. Nam feels her real heart beat a little faster, how it always does when she sees the pod cutting through the water, eight sleek pink acrobats racing and leaping then plunging back under. She knows each of their names, or at least she did last week. The dolphins like to change them, and give each other nicknames, which Nam told them is very Thai of them.

She switches off the motor. Her little boat sloshes forward on the afterkick, drifts. The pod comes closer, squealing and chattering. In her goggles, Nam sees more net-friends joining her, hopeful today will be one of the special days.

Some come from as far away as Nueva Gran Colombia—she visited a paisa girl's goggles once, and marveled at the lush green city with its every spare surface coated in carbon-catch moss. Another comes from Nuuk, the colorful capital of Kalaallit Nunaat where the buildings perch on telescoping legs.

Each person brings a small trickle of netcash, which is how Nam bought her extra nerve suit, and a pair of flutterwings for her littlest sibling's birthday, and any other things that were not voted as food-shelter-health-happiness essentials.

As Truth noses up to the boat, grinning, Nam feels a grin spreading across her own face. "Sawadee," she says. "How are you, Truth?"

Truth is the oldest dolphin in the pod, around forty years old, but still the quickest and most playful. She's always teasing the young calves, swimming upside down beneath them or blowing little air rings at their bellies.

"Squid squid squid," Truth says, her chattering squeal turned to synth-speech by Nam's goggles. "Delicious sea. Nam?"

Nam recognizes the last chirp, even without the synth-speech translation, and it always flutters her stomach to know the pod has given her a name. She reaches back into her cooler and pulls out a few of the freshly caught bobtail squid Truth prefers.

"Here," she says, dropping them into the water. "Would you like to wear the suit today, Truth?"

Truth gobbles down the squid first, then circles the boat, then finally surfaces to squeal her answer. "Suit day! Yes. Yes. Rebarbative suit day!"

Nam blinks—sometimes the babeltech goes far afield with dolphin vocabulary. But the enthusiasm is clear, so she takes the extra nerve suit, the one she dissected and reassembled and waterproofed, and helps web it across Truth's rubbery pink body. The other dolphins swirl around, curious.

"There are 308 net-friends watching," Nam says. "Is that okay?"

"Friends," Truth chitters. "Many swim. Nam swim. All swim."

Nam caps the stream, then sits back in her boat and becomes the 309th. Her heart thrums with anticipation as the nerve suit links up, and then—

Nam is in the water, feeling the cool lap against Truth's blubber-sheathed body, seeing through Truth's low-light eyes. Nam is a good swimmer. She relishes the feel of a perfect stroke, her whole body working in harmony, from her cupped hand biting the surface to her flexed feet knifing through it.

Swimming as a dolphin is that, factor ten. One of the young bulls rockets down toward the seabed and Nam-with-Truth rockets after him, snout pointed for the sandy bottom. She scrapes her belly against the bottom, sends sand swirling everywhere.

Then up, up fast, tail threshing her toward the gauzy sunlight. The bull hurtles clear of the water and Nam-with-Truth does the same trick. There's a beautiful never-ending moment of suspension, up in the sky, shedding the sea off her fins and flukes, perfectly weightless in a cloud of soft shattered glass.

Nam is flying through the air. Nam is lying in her boat. Nam is all around the world, joined to three hundred other electric heartbeats. She knows it should probably feel mythical, like the age of ancient plastic, the age of gas-guzzling planes and freighters crisscrossing the oceans.

But instead, it just feels true.

A WORM TO THE WISE

Marissa Lingen

AUGUSTA LEARNED NOT TO TAKE WORMS FOR GRANTED.

When she moved to the project grounds, she had always felt that worms were something that turned up when it rained and got squashed and made the sidewalk slightly smelly. The idea of a worm swap would have sounded surreal—the idea that she would find herself at one, ridiculous.

And yet there she was in the cool morning of the San Jose outposts, standing over a series of buckets, peering skeptically. The soil in them was rich, dark, wet; even Augusta could see that it was better than the dry grayish stuff she had been divesting of its large chunks of concrete. The reddish brown worms writhed ecstatically through it.

"They're not Alabama jumpers, are they?" she said. "Vicki said we shouldn't bring any of those back, they're bad for the lizards."

Reuben nodded slowly. Augusta waited. She had learned to wait for Reuben, as she had learned to appreciate worms. He was from North Dakota, one parent from Mandan and the other from the Standing Rock Reservation, and talked like he had the time to spend all day to get where he was going. "Not Alabama jumpers," he said, when both Augusta and the owner of the bucket of worms were ready to choke with impatience. "We can have some of those, but not too many. They aerate. These are mostly different kinds of nightcrawlers."

"Good kinds?"

"Good enough," said Reuben, finally looking up. "Depends what she wants for them." Augusta bit back a sigh. This was the cue for Reuben and the woman with the bucket of worms to bargain for another half hour. It was astonishing to her that people with so little could spend so much time arguing about it—and the haggling over the worms was nothing compared to the time she and Reuben had spent back at the project, determining what they had to trade.

Augusta wandered off to look at the worm-seller's farm. Reuben acknowledged this with a nod, silently agreeing to meet up later. She wished that she could take notes on the spot, pages and pages of notes, on what was offered, what the other people at the meetup looked like, all colors but mostly sun-lined, all shapes and sizes, far more ages than she had expected. How the burnt-out remnants of the bulldozed houses framed and outlined the space they could set up in. How the farm had adapted itself around the wreckage. But that would blow her cover. She contented herself with trying to remember as much as she could until she was back in the privacy of her cubicle.

When the buses stopped going to the cheaper housing in southern Santa Clara, Augusta had to leave Stanford, scholarships notwithstanding. Fuel cost too much to pick up diminished handfuls of struggling people from the outskirts—but fuel cost too much for anyone in her neighborhood to own a car, either.

Her advisor had shrugged. "To be honest, journalism degrees aren't worth what they used to be," she'd said. "If you really want this—if you still really want this, even now—" And she'd peered at Augusta to make sure the meaning was clear. Now, after the Big One, and all the Little Ones with it. Now, since the market had gone haywire. Now, with the weather doing whatever strange things it might, in some random order that no longer resembled the clear wet season/dry season of Northern California past. All the giant pile of now.

Augusta had only ever wanted to be a journalist. To tell the truth where it was most needed, she thought. "I still do."

Her advisor had nodded. "Your main chance is to come up with your own story. To research and write it, freelance. Something eye-catching, something with a great pitch. That's how careers are made these days. Like in the frontier days, I guess. Show them what you can do. And then do another. And another."

How she was to eat while she was "showing them" was left as an exercise for the student.

Augusta might have given up and taken an indenture with one of the corporations that hung around and picked up young people hungry for contracts, if not for Skyler. Skye had been her freshman roommate, and they'd tolerated each other amiably, Skye's passion of the week and Augusta's cool detachment rubbing up against each other well enough to live together, if not a friendship of ages.

So when Skye said she was going to join a soil reclamation project in the South Bay, she didn't expect Augusta to offer to join her—but she didn't seem surprised, either. Other options weren't thick on the ground.

Skye had lasted a week. Augusta was still there.

She had not expected a bulldozed housing development with shards of McMansions around her. She wasn't sure what she *had* expected. Something idyllic and green and earnest. Something bucolic.

They had the earnest part, at least.

The Hayward hills had always been prone to fire, but when the housing developments dwindled to a few people, most of the yards went unwatered. An earthquake triggered a huge fire, killing thirty of the people still living in the developments, including five children under school age. Horrified, the South Bay suburban governments vowed that they wouldn't go the way of the East Bay. The largely abandoned communities were evacuated and bulldozed. Property values had fallen far enough that no one wanted to maintain the rest.

Enter Vicki and Reuben and the rest of their group, gathered around them as they worked. The bulldozers left depleted soil and giant masses of concrete in their wake—plus invasive species and the debris that didn't quite make it to the dump trucks. It was a mess. It was good solid work for as many people as they could get to do it. By the time Augusta got there, the first patch of soil had even been restored enough to make a large credible vegetable garden.

Vicki, the broad-shouldered, dreadlocked head of the project, had put them to work hauling chunks of concrete in wheelbarrows. The project gave them sledgehammers, work gloves, and a pep talk; all power was human power when they could manage it. Their job—alongside half a dozen other project members—was to pull chunks of concrete and toss them into a designated shell of a basement down the block. The remaining soil could then be worked, fertilized—restored, as much as possible, to the fertile farmland that had predated the flawed development.

It was a great theory, except that it involved Augusta herself hauling concrete for hours at a time. Despite the work gloves and boots she'd brought with her from Stanford, she ended each day bruised and exhausted. She barely had the energy to make notes on her handheld for her story—and yet if not in-depth investigative reporting, what was she there for?

In the early days, she hoped for a scandal. Hypocrisy would be best—environmentalists who used polluting technology for literally anything, that was always a popular way to make the public feel better about itself. If not that, a titillating exposé of latter-day hippie life would do. Orgies around bonfires, drug use, sordid abuse of petty power—that kind of story was easy to spread on social media. It would make a name for her.

After two weeks of crushing labor with never an orgy in sight, not even a bonfire, and considerably less drug use than she'd seen at Stanford, Augusta found that the kind of story she was planning shifted. Not to a puff piece, she assured herself. Not becoming the soil reclamation PR department. Just . . . not raking the same kind of muck.

She began to wonder whether the people who came up with the term *muckraking* had ever spent much time working soil with a rake. It sounded so easy until you did it.

That night Augusta had finished with her notes, or what she could make herself do of her notes, and was lying on her bed in her narrow cubicle, staring at the ceiling. The person in the next cubicle was playing the guitar, badly. The A string was slightly sharp, and it threw everything off.

It was, she thought, the closest thing to a scandal she'd uncovered: the idea that someone might have paid for guitar lessons and only gotten this little value out of them.

A tap on her door interrupted both her thoughts and the guitar noodling. It was Vicki. "Just wanted to check in and see how you feel like you're settling in with us, since you decided to stay when your friend left."

Augusta put a social smile on her face. "I'm pretty sore. But it's going okay, I think."

"Glad to hear it. If you've never used arnica for bruises, we've got some in the medicine chest. A lot of new people haven't, but hauling concrete around . . . well, you get good at scrapes and bruises."

"Thanks," said Augusta. She tried to think what she would say if she was a passionate young environmentalist. "Good worms we got today?"

Vicki grinned. "I think so. It's a start, at least. We'll just keep feeding them and see how it goes."

Even before the weather had shifted, there had been no winter that *was* a winter, in the South Bay. Rains, and those still came, but no cold snap, nothing that would end the work and send them scuttling inside like the bugs and worms they cultivated.

Augusta found herself still around for the feast they put on for themselves for Labor Day. And more, she found herself trusted. The urge to wander off from Reuben's slow bargains evaporated, and in its place grew the desire to make sure he was getting the best bargain he could from the sellers of muck and creatures.

As a result, there came a day when she was proud to hear from Vicki, "What great lice, Reuben! Wow, what a find."

"Not me, Augusta," said Reuben, smiling at both of them.

Augusta expected Vicki to be surprised. Instead, Vicki beamed at her and said, "See, I knew you'd get the hang of it. We need more helpers. You get that now."

For a moment Augusta thought Vicki meant herself and other new recruits. But no, she was bending over the box of woodlice, cooing over them in dotty tones.

Augusta wished she could take a picture without tipping them off. This was just the sort of thing that the few people who paid for freelance journalism these days would eat up: the wacky hippies hugging their bugs. She turned away from Vicki's enthusiasm, feeling a little sour about even thinking of it. Augusta had been excited about the woodlice herself.

Dangers of going undercover, she thought. Self-portrait of the journalist as a louse enthusiast. The important part was whether she could think how to make a reader excited about woodlice. They just looked like any other lightly armored bug, a little scuttling thing she would not want to find under a rock. Except now she would. How did that change? It certainly wasn't because of the joy and beauty of seeing them up close. Woodlouse encounters would not help.

By Thanksgiving she was instructing a few new recruits on how long their showers could last and where to put their work boots, and Vicki was confiding in her. Augusta tried to maintain a sense of journalistic detachment, but it was very hard when someone she lived with day in and day out showed up with cider and complaints.

"No one takes us seriously," said Vicki, a great deal less sober than Augusta had ever seen her. She was sitting on the floor of Augusta's cubicle. Augusta kept the bed for herself, feeling more confident that she wouldn't spill cider all over it.

"Oh, I don't know," she said carefully.

Vicki took another deep drink from her bottle of cider, shaking her head.

Augusta ventured, "I think they just . . . they just don't know what we're doing. Why it should matter."

"No, no. They already think it doesn't. If you manufacture fertilizer, that's a valid job," said Vicki, blowing her bangs off her forehead. "People pay you for it individually. But if you make the soil healthier, if you make the soil live again, it benefits everyone and is paid for by no one. No one wants you to do it, they just want it to happen invisibly. They even resent it when you do."

"I think . . ." Augusta hesitated.

"No, go ahead."

"I think that they only see it as a means to an end. That if you're making the soil healthier, you should be doing it so that *you* can grow *your* crops in *your* soil. Or even so that *you* can have a nice garden in *your* yard. But *your* neighborhood, *your* ecosystem . . . no one is supposed to feel possessive about that. No one is supposed to work for that."

"*Your* planet," Vicki muttered. "Yeah. Yeah."

"So . . . how do we change that? What if someone could get the message out to people who just . . . don't know what's going on around them? Who have never had to pay attention?"

"Never pay attention," Vicki muttered, and Augusta realized that this was probably not the time for a serious discussion.

"We can talk about this in the morning," said Augusta softly. "I really want to help."

But when morning came, Vicki—apparently none the worse for wear—was talking about bacteria testing, good bacteria, bad bacteria, balanced bacteria. She seemed focused, and Augusta didn't want to interfere with that focus.

Or else she was being a coward. But the bacteria question was interesting. She knew that there were quite functional ways to transfer beneficial gut bacteria from one human to another through fecal transplant; would that work with dirt? Or with manure? Was someone near them willing and able to test what bacteria their manure was likely to have?

That night she used her handheld to research it. It took her a few false starts to get to the really useful information about soil—alarming things showed up under her first few searches about poop and bacteria—but eventually she got there. The time she would usually have spent making notes for the story that kept receding beyond her fingertips went into reading about dung tests.

She was riveted.

The next day she brought a plan to the group about how they could get goat manure from a group across the bay in exchange for some of their own sheep manure, and that would enrich both soil biomes.

"How do you know that?" said Reuben.

"I've read papers on it. Eight different papers. I'll send you the links."

He nodded with what she hoped was grudging respect, or maybe even just respect. It was hard to tell with Reuben.

* * *

Augusta couldn't afford to get to her parents' for Christmas and New Year's, but her college advisor had invited several former students for the holiday supper, and she could catch a ride with one of the newer project members who was originally from Atherton and whose parents didn't mind dropping her off. The number of electric lights in her advisor's house now felt jarring, dazzling after the sparse lighting of the soil-project housing.

All the other former students had corporate jobs. Augusta privately wondered whether it was depressing for her advisor to teach journalism but apparently not any journalists. When she was asked about what she was doing, she found herself telling them a great deal about fungi, which ones were wanted and which might be destructive. The other former students put on polite listening faces, but Augusta's advisor leaned in, chin in hands.

"I never knew you were so interested in mycorrhizal interactions," Augusta said to her as they were saying goodbye.

"I never knew *you* were, and that's the important part." Her advisor folded her arms and surveyed Augusta. "When you're ready, I think you'll have something here. Something a little different, maybe. The science press? No, that's not it, they already know all this. Something for the general public *about* the science of it, though. That's not for every venue, but there are still some. Come to me when you have it ready."

"Thank you," said Augusta, and hugged her impulsively. But she spent the ride back wondering if she *would* ever have anything ready. None of the notes had made their way into prose. She was barely thinking about it at all anymore. Was there even a story? Her advisor seemed to think so, but she had gotten much more immersed in the story of what color the dirt was turning, how it felt when a spade bit into it.

Not many days into the new year, Augusta led a group of new volunteers out to their latest site—only to find that it was now across the street from a plastic fence enclosing some of the land they'd spent the most time on.

"What's *that*," said one of the newbies, and Augusta pursed her lips and said, "Run and get Vicki."

The fence went on for quite some ways, so it took them time to find the notice pinned to it saying exactly *who* would be parceling off this newly rich land for sale to people who wanted small farms there.

"But they can't, it's ours," said Augusta.

Vicki made a face.

"It *is* ours, isn't it?"

"We can talk about this tonight."

Augusta poured herself into hauling concrete fragments, though she had the seniority for more complex tasks. The sheer physical labor was what she needed to deal with being scared, angry, confused, anything else that came up. Physically exhausted was better than all of those things. Physically exhausted was reliable.

So when she confronted Vicki after dinner, she managed not to do it at the top of her lungs. "Why didn't you answer me, whether this land is ours? I thought it was ours. I never thought we were doing this for some corporation."

Vicki's chin jutted out. "We're not! And we won't. It's just . . . complicated."

"*How* is it *complicated*?" Complicated sounded like a scandal, and Augusta realized she had stopped wanting one of those months ago.

Reuben put his hand on her shoulder—she had not realized he was even there. "Squatters' rights," he said in his usual succinct way.

Augusta turned to Vicki, who nodded. "This land has been abandoned. We checked out the laws, and if you live on land for five years, it's yours. There are some other rules, but that's the gist. Especially if you've worked it and the previous owners left hazards on it, which you *know* they did, you've seen all the jagged shards of foundations."

"But they think—"

"They think we won't have the money for lawyers. So we have to figure out how to have the money for lawyers." Vicki sighed. "We'll have to prove that we were living on this whole section of land, not just the narrowly defined area where the buildings are. We'll have to prove . . . I mean, I don't even know why I'm saying this, I don't know where we'll get the money, and proof isn't always the point, sometimes it's public support. I hate to say it, but it's true."

"We all know," said Reuben.

"I know you do, you've all worked so hard, I'm so sorry . . ."

Augusta took a deep breath. "What if there was something we could do about public support?"

Both of them looked at her intently. "Absolutely, what?" said Vicki.

"I . . . I came here under false pretenses. I'm sorry. I'm a journalist—well, a journalism student—well, I *wanted* to be a journalist. And this was going to be my exposé. Except I got here and there wasn't anything to expose. And . . . and I liked it."

Neither of them responded. Augusta plowed on. "So . . . my old advisor told me she could help me get a piece published. About this place, about what we're doing here. She heard me at Christmas, talking about fungus and stuff, and she thought . . ." Augusta paused to think. "She might have thought all along that a deeper approach would be better. Rather than scandal-mongering. But she let me go figure out what was here, what to talk about. I haven't written anything yet. I stopped taking notes a few months ago. But if that would help . . ."

She held her breath. Would they kick her out for being a spy all along? She would miss the woodlice. She would miss the worms. She would not miss the concrete even a little, but that was sort of the point.

Instead, Reuben nodded. "Sounds good, get the word out."

"I'm not . . . I can't do a PR puff piece," Augusta said. "No one would accept it, and also I won't."

He cocked his head. "No, I wouldn't expect so."

"Even if it's not," said Vicki. "I mean, of course it's not, of course you have . . ." She waved her hand. "Journalistic integrity or whatever. No, this is good work, Augusta, we need this."

"But I . . ." Augusta felt like the world was spinning. "I don't want to launch a journalism career. I thought I did. But I don't."

"Okay," said Reuben cheerfully.

"But we need it!"

Vicki and Reuben looked at each other. "Sit down, hon," said Vicki.

Augusta felt like a kindergartener, but she sat.

"What do you want?" Vicki asked, and apparently something in Augusta's face made her hold up a hand and say, "No, really, what do you *want*?"

Augusta crumpled. "I want to mess with worms."

Reuben laughed. "Good!"

"It's just . . . I really like it. I really like the work, I really like seeing the difference from one week to another."

"Okay." Vicki nodded. "Okay, good, keep doing it."

"But this is not what I thought I was doing!" said Augusta. This time they both laughed, and Augusta scowled at them and tried again. "This is not who I thought I *was*."

Vicki patted her shoulder. "I thought I was going to be a doctor."

"My *mother* thought I was going to be an electrical engineer," said Reuben.

"Okay, but that's your mother," said Vicki, making a face,

reminding Augusta that she was still new here and didn't know all the jokes and references. "Everyone comes from somewhere. We knew that. You weren't here to sabotage the work. That's what matters, doing the work. Do you think you'll be okay if you do both? If you mostly mess with worms but sometimes write stories about us?"

"I . . . I think so. I can try."

Vicki grinned. "Hey, that's all we can ever do."

The wave of relief that crashed over Augusta was exhausting. She slept past the morning breakfast call for the first time in her months at the project, and through the morning work call too. She woke up dazed and found everyone else already out working. This *was* her new work, though, so she went and stuck her head in the rain barrel and got down to it.

Or tried. She wanted to write a gentle article about worms in wet soil, about turning manure into gray crumbled earth and watching it come back to life, about the smell of the sweat of a dozen people who had been working for the same things as you. She got the last part in, but it came out angrier. Furious at the labor that was being stolen. Instead of earth, she wrote fire.

She convinced herself to show it to Vicki at supper. Instead of sighing over its failure—or even critiquing it—Vicki nodded. "Good, okay. Write the next one."

"The next one?"

"Get your pitches out, write the next one. Come on, you knew this would take more than one."

Augusta had never whined about blisters on her palms from hauling concrete. She wanted to whine about the prospect of typing. "I don't know how many contacts my advisor has."

"So let's find out. Figure out what you can tell the rich people's gardening magazines. The zoologists. Whoever. And when you're done with that, start again at the same places, with pieces on the rest of the movement. You didn't think that you were going to be our fairy godjournalist and fix it in an article, did you?"

"No, of course not. No. But . . . I don't know anything about the rest of the movement," Augusta said, but she was wavering.

"Good," said Vicki, as if she'd come right out and said yes. "You can learn. This is going to be a long fight. But if we have someone talking to the world from inside the tent instead of outside . . ."

"We should get another tent," said Reuben, and they argued about it until Augusta got bored and wandered off to help with patching the roof, doing the dishes, all the things that inevitably needed doing for the world to keep turning.

A SÉANCE IN THE ANTHROPOCENE

Abigail Larkin

GRANDMA MARNE WAS THE ONE WHO TOLD WILLA THAT THE world was once powered by ghosts.

"The oil. The coal. It all came from ancient things, dead things dug out of the Earth."

Willa was raised to hold a healthy skepticism of extraordinary claims.

"No way."

"Yes way."

"Like, dinosaurs?"

"Well, no," Marne said. She set down her gardening shears and stood up, wiping her brow. To a layman, the garden around their home looked wicked and untamed. A mess of tangled gamagrass spilled out between trellises of tumbling vines; tomato plants heavy with fruit—most green, but some blushing red already—nestled among sprays of peppermint and bloodroot and bee balm. But Willa knew that the garden was a system designed with scrupulous care, and everything down to the very last leaf was in its place. Milkweed to attract pollinators. Garlic and pennyroyal to repel pests. Marne Wynne was a scientist, and she brought a scientist's mind to all endeavors.

Grandma Marne stood back, surveying her kingdom with a sharp eye, and found it to her liking.

"The dinosaurs came much later," she explained. "The oil came from small organisms—algae and zooplankton that existed millions of years ago when all this was still an ocean."

Willa imagined the big machines she had seen in books and movies drilling into the ground, opening up a hole of black carnage, unleashing millions of angry spirits into the sky.

"I like our way better," she said, picking a ripe blackcap from a nearby bush and popping it in her mouth. It was sun-warmed and sweet.

Grandma Marne laughed. "So do I."

They had then gone inside, where they made blackberry jam. They sealed the jars with steam and stored them in the root cellar, so later, when the berries were out of season, they could still have the taste of summer in pies or spread over fresh bread or even straight from the spoon. But the story of the old way lingered in Willa's mind. She thought of the oil and coal ghosts—the way they roiled the world and pushed life on Earth to the brink, the countless victims of their vengeance. Had they ever been properly put to rest?

Years later, this memory percolated in her mind as she pitched her idea for her capstone project to Mrs. Menendez, her academic advisor. As she spoke, Mrs. Menendez riffled through the holodoc displayed above her desk, then looked up over the frames of her lime-green readers.

"I'm not sure I follow," she said, "You want to write a book for your project? A history?"

"Essentially," Willa replied.

"But surely this already exists. Your capstone's contribution to the community has to be novel. Otherwise, you won't pass the year."

"That's the thing—there are a ton of books written about the technical aspects of the Realignment, the upheaval of the twenty-first century, the suits against OPEC and oligarchs." She took a deep breath. She had practiced this speech in front of her bathroom mirror all week. "But I want to write something from a more human angle. Informed by firsthand testimony—people who lived through it, who remember the Dark Decade or maybe even filling up their personal vehicles with gasoline."

Mrs. Menendez grimaced. "Are there any left?"

"Some."

"You really think they'd be willing to share their stories?"

"I think so."

The counselor flipped through the proposal again.

"I don't know, Willa. This is all rather . . . morbid. I would have thought the granddaughter of Marne Wynne would have come up with a stellar engineering proposal. You have a real advantage, with access to Sunfields Inc. and lots of resources the other students won't have."

Willa sighed. Her grandmother was the founder and CEO of Sunfields, the largest solar farm in North Carolina and the biggest single provider in the Eastern regional grid. She sat on the board of the Triad Energy Alliance and headed the steering committee of the New Army Corps of Engineers. Willa had lived her whole life in her long shadow.

"I understand that perspective. But, respectfully, Mrs. Menendez, I don't want an advantage. I want to make my own way."

Mrs. Menendez bit her lip. Willa could tell she wasn't convinced. She had anticipated this. The Three Tribes Technical Academy of Buncombe County was one of the elite tribal schools established during the Realignment—preeminent among all of the Foundling Schools—and renowned around the world as a technical powerhouse. Prior capstones had yielded improved battery storage capacity, uncovered efficiencies in photovoltaic systems, or found new uses for Class E noncircular materials. Those projects embodied man's highest ideals: ingenuity, resilience, resourcefulness. Hers would hunt its demons.

"The capstone criteria also states that the rationale for the project must be founded upon Cherokee values," Willa continued. "Like storytelling and forging a connection to our past."

She sat up straighter and spoke from her gut, the way Grandma Marne taught her. "My classmates have fabulous engineering ideas. This will be different. Unique. Please, I have a really clear vision for it."

Mrs. Menendez seemed to be sizing her up. Then she cocked her head to the side and said, "Alright, Willa, I'll sign off on this. But you better know what you're doing. Your future is at stake here."

Jumping up from her chair, Willa shook Mrs. Menendez's hand. "I promise, you won't be disappointed!"

Willa had been so busy researching her project that she had completely forgotten about Atonement Ceremony. Her mom rapped on her bedroom door and told her to be ready for the gathering in ten minutes. Willa swore, powered down her desk, and pulled out the black jumpsuit from her wardrobe.

On the walk to the town green, she saw Phil. He looked somber, dressed in black, quiet, reflective. That was the point of Atonement Ceremony. But it meant more for the Bevins, of course. There were two kinds of scholarship students at the academy—those like Willa, who had roots in the tribe, and those like Phil, whose family's trade had once been in oil or gas or coal. The reservation kids were proud of their heritage—but for folks like Phil, it wasn't something they liked to talk about much. Willa jogged up next to him.

"*Osiyo*, Phil," she said.

"*Osiyo*, Wynne."

"Don't act like you didn't see Baltimore skewer Pittsburgh last night."

He groaned. "I was hoping you didn't."

"I'm happy to change out our names on the kitchen duties schedule for you."

"The way this season's going, I'll be scrubbing dishes till I'm as old as my great-granddad." He grinned, but Willa couldn't help but notice that it seemed strained.

When they arrived at the green, Principal Chief Batista was already at the center lectern with a few other councilmen. At the minute of sunset, his voice boomed across the field through nearly invisible speakers hovering overhead.

"Welcome," he said, "to the Forty-Sixth National Atonement Ceremony. Today is bittersweet. All across the country, we honor those who shepherded us through the Dark Decade. Those who remade the world." Willa stole a glance at Grandma Marne, who sat at the center lectern with a few other elders. Her face was impassive. "But we also remember the world we lost."

Behind him, a stereopticon powered on. A whale swirled in the air, flipping its massive flukes.

"The world we lost to willful ignorance and greed."

Behind the chief played the iconic footage of the Manhattan drownings. People in the crowd shook their heads and clicked their tongues as the buildings that couldn't be saved were demolished and crumbled into the swollen Hudson River. In the twilight, Willa saw Phil gazing at the ground.

"We renew our commitment to channel our *utalawuhska*—our rage against the past—to build a more righteous future on behalf of those who perished."

The stereopticon changed again, and a coastline-altering hurricane swept away homes in one gust. Then again: refugees huddled in an encampment outside Poughkeepsie. And again: people lining up around blocks for food rations. And again: the drowning of Miami, Brooklyn, New Orleans. California hills on fire. Boats crammed with screaming migrants sinking into a boiling sea. Riots as soldiers fired guns into crowds. And then: bird upon mouse upon frog upon fish, in endless procession, species that Willa had never seen—would never see—except in pictures and videos, until the images seemed to blur.

If she looked hard, she could see through the screen to the glowing faces on the opposite lawn. If she listened, she could hear the cicadas starting to sing.

Grandma Marne was the first person Willa interviewed for her project. She booted up her desk as Grandma Marne, wrapped in a traditional shawl, poured them both a cup of sassafras tea sweetened with honey from the apiary.

"Do you mind if I record?" Willa asked.

Grandma Marne shook her head. Just as she had set up the mic, a crow outside the window shrieked. Grandma Marne rolled her eyes, rose, and shut a window to stem the noise. "He's been out there every day for weeks now. Doesn't know how to shut up," she said. She sat again and cupped her mug of tea. "Used to be more than just crows, you know. All kinds of birds, each with her own song. You wouldn't believe the music—a symphony every morning. It's funny, I can't remember when it stopped." She looked out the window.

What a beautiful thing to let slip through our fingers, Willa thought. How could it have happened? She wanted so badly to understand.

Grandma Marne turned back and smiled. "So what would you like to know?"

"I guess we can go chronologically," Willa said. "What do you remember about the Dark Decade?"

"Hmm. It was a hard time. I was just a little girl, and like so many back then, all we could afford was canned goods and non-perishables. I think that spurred my interest in organic garden-ing. I didn't have a green thing for a year." She paused, looking thoughtful. "Though I do still have a thing for La Choy."

"How did you get by?"

Marne shrugged, "We did okay. It was a shock, though. Lots of things leading up to the Dark Decade happened gradually, but the food shortage happened all at once. We led very different lives before." She lowered her voice. "I remember a time when stores stocked more food than you could ever imagine. And if it didn't sell by a certain date, they would just *throw it away*."

Willa looked up from her notes in disbelief.

"Why would they do something like that?"

Grandma Marne shrugged. "They thought they'd never run out, I guess. Anyway, we weren't a people who were used to hard-ship or scarcity. So when all of a sudden a middle-class family couldn't afford a bunch of bananas . . ."

"It was bad."

Marne nodded grimly. "Eventually, they had to ration everything. One time, I went to the store with my mother, and the man handing out groceries said something in passing, like, 'Lucky you, you got the last bag of coffee.' The man behind us got angry and demanded we give it to him. Mom refused, and the employees and other shoppers backed her up—but then the man followed her outside."

Willa's stomach clenched at the thought. "What did you do?"

"We ran. I flung myself inside our car, and the next thing I knew, he was banging on the window. Mom just drove. I was terrified that he would come after us. When we finally parked in our driveway, I was so relieved, but my mother started sobbing—turns out she had dropped the groceries in the parking lot."

Willa turned all this over in her mind. "So around then we made big changes to the energy mix."

"Not exactly."

"*No?*" Willa was flabbergasted.

"It wasn't until around the third year of famine that a critical mass of people recognized the problem had to be more than a fluke. Only then did people demand the end of fossil fuels—and our problems had only just begun. We hadn't invested enough in energy alternatives, so once we pulled the plug on fossils, the grid became unreliable even as energy costs went up."

Willa paused before she said, "But then the Realignment got going, and things improved."

"Well, yes. But at the time nothing seemed certain—nobody was sure we were on the right path."

"What do you mean?"

"Well, take the Foundling Schools, for example. Now, it seems inevitable—but it wasn't an easy choice. It's hard to imagine now, but back then, Indigenous lands were mostly poor and struggling. It became about more than training workers to service the grid— we wanted to disrupt the cycle of poverty. But to many, it seemed like we were benefiting some at the expense of others. Others thought fossil fuel workers and their children unworthy of the opportunity. Hadn't they gotten us into this mess? Why should they get a break? Still more thought it was exploitative to take students away from their families. That really divided the tribe. Sending Native children to what would essentially be a boarding school was . . . a loaded concept."

Willa paused, then said, "Well, it's a good thing those people didn't get their way."

"They didn't go down without a fight. Some of the detractors threw stones at me and my classmates as we walked to our classes. Some of those people were Cherokee. That was the most painful for me."

Willa reached across the table and squeezed her hand.

Grandma Marne smiled. "It's ancient history."

"So how were we able to move forward?"

She seemed to ponder the question. "I'm not sure I know the answer to that." She poured herself some more tea from the clay pot. "It could have easily gone the other way, in my view."

Willa felt the tug of *utalawuhska* in her chest. "They waited *so long* to act! People could have done something sooner, and they chose not to. They were so blind. And so many suffered because of it."

Grandma Marne looked at her for a second, then got up from her chair and moved to a desk by a window. She took something out of a drawer and placed it on the table.

Willa's eyes widened. "Is that—"

Grandma Marne nodded. "Coal. Anthracite, really. The industry tried to brand it as 'clean coal' before its downfall."

"Where did you get it?"

"One of my teachers worked at a port. A shipment was delivered one of his last days there—but by then, its value had dropped so low, nobody came for it. The buyers just left it there. He picked some up as a souvenir. Gave this piece to me."

Willa held it in her hand—it was hard, shiny, glimmering like some kind of Horcrux. She thought she could feel the thrum of the spirits that clung to it.

"Keep it," Grandma Marne said, "as a talisman."

Willa didn't know if she wanted to keep it, but she slipped it inside her satchel. She didn't want her grandmother to feel bad.

"*Wado*, Grandma."

Willa arrived at the Asheville Amerorail station at nine o'clock with a small backpack, a thermos of black coffee, and a tin of cornbread and jam that her grandmother had insisted she take with her. She always felt invigorated when traveling by Amerorail.

The train was called the Needle because of the way it threaded through the countryside wildlife crossings, gathering the land like fabric gathered on a needle and thread. The crossings were designed to allow forests to migrate overhead—slow, giant, singular organisms moving across time.

Willa settled herself in a compartment and soaked in the moment. It was her first time on the rail by herself. She felt like an adult—utterly prepared and on-schedule. She gazed out the window, watching meadows and barns streak by in flashes as they passed under the hills, like watercolor stop-motion. Then she booted up her desk and busied herself with some reading and breakfast. In a little under an hour and a half, the Needle glided into Union Station. She marched through the main hall and ogled the high, arched ceiling stamped with golden florets, the sounds of heels on tile click-clacking all over. She checked in at her hostel room, which was little more than a bed and small workspace—she was allotted a small travel stipend for her project, but she had budgeted to stretch it as far as it would go. Then she spent the rest of the day at the National Archives.

Hours passed in a blur of newspaper headlines, video testimonials, digital archives. By the time she left the din of the atrium, the morning's glow had been replaced by exhaustion. She decided to take a break, and when she stepped out into the balmy D.C. air, she felt as if she had emerged from underwater.

The bleakest events of the Dark Decade were catastrophic—the dissolution of governments in the Caribbean, Micronesia, the

Philippines, Bangladesh. The refugees who found no respite in a world reeling from famine and economic collapse. The children who went hungry. The species that went extinct.

But the rosy stories about the way things used to be—stories she had come across almost by mistake—touched her in a way that was difficult to describe. A man's account of his boyhood in a drowned place called Martha's Vineyard, for example, where he once saw a blue whale off the side of his uncle's fishing boat. "He came right up to me," the man had said, "he really did! I reached out and touched his back, and I swear he was looking right up at me, sizing me up, see? Trynta figure out what I was made of. It was wild. You should have been there."

It wasn't loss that she felt. Martha's Vineyard and blue whales were things that had never—would never—be hers. You can't lose what you never had. Was it *utalawuhska*? Rage against the past? *Righteous* anger?

Perhaps.

As she climbed into her bed later that evening, she vowed that she would channel this feeling into her project. To make sense of the past—to shape the future, even. She'd do it for her grandmother, who might have once believed that she would one day see a whale.

That night, her dreams were haunted by phantom giants, lost to the blackness of the sea.

Phil's great-grandfather lived on the other side of town in a little square house made of yellow pine in a row of little square houses made of pine. She had been looking forward to this interview, but now that the moment had arrived, her nerves jangled and her palms felt moist. She rubbed them on her shorts, ignoring the part of her that wanted to turn around and go home. She felt the chill of ghosts at her back. The lives unlived. The whales. The dead drawn up from their resting places and burned. Didn't they deserve answers? Didn't she?

She knocked on the door. A dog barked. She heard some scuffling, and then Mr. Bevin was standing at the threshold. His face looked like it was carved from an oak stump. His teeth were yellow and his beard and hair as white and wispy as spun sugar. But his eyes were sharp, a relic untouched by age.

"Good to meet you, Willa." He outstretched a broad hand and she shook it. "I'm Paul Bevin. This is Carly."

A little white dog scampered over and planted two paws on Willa's shins—she weighed almost nothing. Willa returned the greeting with a scratch on the head.

Mr. Bevin grinned, and his smile was like a gash. He gestured inside the house, and Willa followed him into a dim living room, taking a seat on one of three squashy armchairs. He offered her a dusty-looking hard candy from a dish, which she declined.

"How can I help you?" he asked, popping one of the hard candies into his mouth.

Willa explained the concept behind her capstone. Mr. Bevin nodded, listening intently.

"I'm trying to get a range of testimony for the project, and, well, there aren't many people left from your generation who—ah—"

"Mined coal?"

"Right."

"Well, what would you like to know?"

There were so many things she wanted to know, but she decided to start easy.

"What was it like working for Fox Fuels?"

Mr. Bevin scratched his beard and looked off. "Boring, for the most part. We were one of the last operational coal mines in the country. By then most of the job was automated. I was one of the stragglers who hung on. Mostly did administrative work, but occasionally conducted inspections of the equipment, went down into the mines."

"What were the mines like?"

He grunted. "Dark. Big hole in the ground. Nothing to write home about."

For a moment, silence buzzed about them. Carly trotted around the armchairs and sat at Mr. Bevin's feet. He picked her up, set her in his lap, and said nothing. The room was dusty and suffocating. The silence rolled on, and Willa squirmed until she couldn't hold back any longer.

"Did you know what it was doing? The burning of the coal?"

"You mean to ask, did I willingly poison the Earth?" He chuckled, and Willa felt her insides freeze at the sound.

"If the shoe fits."

He stopped laughing and sighed.

"I'm sorry, I didn't mean to sound flippant." He looked down at his dog and scratched her behind the ears. "You'd think ninety-nine years would be long enough to shake off your petty insecurities. But I suppose I still get a bit defensive about certain things."

"So did you know about the carbon pollution? The climate shift?" Willa repeated.

"Of course we knew," he said. "Everyone knew."

"How did that affect your attitude toward the job?"

He paused for a moment, thinking.

"Do you want to know the honest truth? It affected my attitude very little. Almost not at all."

Willa felt like jumping out of her chair.

"Why?" she finally asked.

"Of course," he said, "I just didn't see what all that had to do with me."

It took a second for Willa to remember to close her mouth. Not even as the oceans rose. As millions of sea creatures washed up dead on beaches. As floods washed away all the wheat and corn in the Midwest and people around the world starved and the old cities drowned. "I'm sorry," she said. "I don't understand that."

He leaned forward in his chair, and Carly leaped down onto the floor.

"Listen," he said. "I don't expect you to understand. But you came here to talk to me, so I assume you want to hear what I have to say. By the time I'd gotten into mining, human-caused climate shift was pretty much common knowledge. That being said, the full extent of the fallout hadn't yet become obvious. Now, you can say that we should have done something *before* it started getting bad—and you would be right. But at the time, the consequences of what would happen seemed insubstantial compared to our insatiable need for energy. That isn't something to discount. Do you think I'd have been mining coal if people weren't buying up electricity generated by Fox Fuels? Everyone was using our energy. Even the Greens and the activists. Even the politicians who insisted that we needed to be shut down. Was I more culpable than they were for what happened? I was giving them what they needed, wasn't I?"

Willa felt stiff. Unyielding. "Why did you choose that profession?"

He laughed bitterly. "By the end, I wished to God I had picked something else. We were punted around like footballs. One day, our jobs were safe, the next, we were told to start looking elsewhere."

"Weren't there job-retraining programs?"

"Eventually. I was open to that. But I think the way we were initially approached turned a lot of people off. Dragged things out longer than it had to be."

"How so?"

He got up and walked around the chairs to a bar where he poured himself a cup of iced tea from a glass pitcher. He offered her a cup, but she shook her head even though her mouth was as dry as the desert.

"Well, there was no acknowledgment that we were being asked to make a sacrifice. Like I said, I would have worked for a solar or wind farm. The old-timers had more trouble. They were already established in their careers, and moving to a new company with a new product—well, it was tough. And we were treated as if we should be groveling on bended knees for the privilege."

He took a long drink from his glass and set it down on the bar with a clink.

"You asked me why I picked mining as a career. I suppose because it was what was available to me. But I grew a community through that place. We offered something useful to people. We were proud of that," he continued. "And you asked me how I felt about the product. The coal. I know it's taboo to say these days, but despite the side effects, I'm grateful for the stuff. It made a lot of things possible for me. It put food on my table, my daughter through school. It was hard to reconcile, you know, it being so harmful to the environment. Anyway, boo-hoo, right," he said, then took another swig of tea. "You sure you don't want any?"

This time, Willa relented, and he passed her a glass. It was cold and bitter.

Willa stared outside the train window, watching the landscape, thick and green, until suddenly, it gave way to silver, amber, and chartreuse. They were passing through a Sunfields solar farm. The artificial trees stretched upward, soaking in photo-voltaic energy that would power nearly everything on the Southeastern grid.

Don't bother trying to improve Mother Nature's design—that was Grandma Marne's philosophy. In rethinking the solar panel as a tree, she had not only made them more effective, but gentler on the planet. In theory, they could be "planted" anywhere, without having to raze an acre of woodland. Of course, in reality, it was more economical to group them in single high-sun locations. But even then, Grandma Marne had envisioned them as a forest, an ecosystem. Sunlight was converted to power in the leaves, transformed inside its trunk, transmitted through a complex root system—there were even spaces carved into the bodies for wildlife to nest. It was a Cherokee way of thinking, she said, and that Native people had always been makers and inventors. She said that Willa would be that way too.

The train glided into the Avery Creek station, where she was the only one to disembark. From there, she got into a communal transit vehicle—CTV—and overrode the automatic destination input for a set of natural coordinates. The CTV zipped out of the station and out through the Asheville suburb. She looked out the window and fiddled with her camera lens and took a few practice shots to get accustomed to the controls.

When the CTV slowed to a stop, Willa stepped outside into the middle of a grassy field. She'd have to walk the rest of the way, but she could already see her final destination. Across a land bridge through a churning offshoot of the Tahkeeosteh River was what remained of North Carolina's last coal-fired power plant.

Willa ignored a sign posted that warned DANGER: KEEP OUT, squeezing past a segment of a fence that had fallen in. She surveyed her surroundings, snapping photos as she went. It had once been a large compound, but almost everything had been carried away long ago. The concrete was cracked and riddled with scrappy weeds. To one side, there was a large steel drum. She didn't know enough about old power plants to know what it was used for. Past that was the station itself.

It was the very same plant to which Fox Fuels would have shipped its inventory. Perhaps Mr. Bevin had come here to meet with utility personnel back in the day. Then, it would have housed massive heavy machinery, but it had long since been hollowed out. The sun streamed in through giant empty window panes, filling up the belly of the station with golden beams. Tendrils of ivy snaked up its walls. Air moved through it as if it breathed. She started as something moved behind her—a fox scrabbling up a pile of rubble from a caved-in wall. It turned to stare at her for a moment. Before she could think to photograph him, he disappeared.

This place, she realized, was alive. Despite a faint rancid smell she noticed only briefly, the plant had been reclaimed. Nature is resilient, she thought. *We* are resilient.

Principal Chief Batista had said during Atonement Ceremony that we must channel our *utalawuhska* to ensure that we never repeat our mistakes. But maybe *utalawuhska* is only half of the equation. Given the past, how do we live in the present? Can we allow ourselves to do so with joy and gratitude? What would that be called?

Nudahvundiyv, she decided. Kindness toward the past.

Willa dug through her satchel. The anthracite Grandma Marne had given her blinked and glimmered. It felt strangely satisfying to hold in her hand. Kneeling, she dug a small hole, where she placed the anthracite and whatever spirits it contained. Then she covered it and said a short prayer.

"*Wado*. I am grateful. You're free now."

She stood there a moment longer. Then she made her way back to the CTV, and home.

THE TREE IN THE BACK YARD

Michelle Yoon

MARISKA LOOKED AT THE CHOICE CARDS IN FRONT OF HER, WON-dering if her papa would have preferred *merbau* or *jati* if he had taken the time to choose before he died. Though if he did, he would have chosen something other than this for his final resting place. He had always been a practical man, always taking what he thought was the most logical route. But he was also extremely stubborn and could dig in his heels so deeply that the only person who could convince him to change his mind was himself, or his wife.

If he could have it his way now, he would have gone the way his wife did: burnt to ashes and scattered into the sea.

Mariska finally settled on the *merbau*. It wasn't so much that she liked it more than the other. She chose it because its name started with the letter M. Also, because the *merbau* tree was native to the

Land, though this came much as an afterthought, in case the first reason wasn't valid somehow. The *merbau* was strong, hardy, and "was once the national tree of Malaysia," boasted the choice card.

Mariska sounded the words out loud. Malaysian *merbau*. They felt foreign on her tongue, yet oddly comforting and familiar. It was as if ancestors from generations past had left little crumbs, clues of a native language long swept to the sidelines, used only on such special occasions to do with the dead.

She packed the choice cards back into the little box they came in, careful to put the *merbau* one right on top. Then she made the call.

"Hello," a perky voice answered. "I see you're calling from Water-Lands, North-West region, the Muds area. Am I correct?"

Mariska barely managed a whispered "yes" before the operator continued babbling the rest of Mariska's home address, her voice bouncing off the walls of the room.

"With this call, I believe you have made your decision. Please place all the choice cards back into the box, with your choice of sapling put right on top of the deck. We will be there to collect the box, along with the deceased, very shortly. We thank you for choosing us, but more importantly, the Earth Mother thanks you for choosing to replenish Her after years of pillaging from Her bosom. Have a pleasant day."

Mariska walked up to her papa's body and placed the little box right above his right shoulder. His skin had already started to turn gray, his mouth impossibly frozen into an eternal frown.

"Papa," she whispered near his ear. "Do you think we'll talk again?"

"Greetings," a gentle voice interrupted. Mariska turned to see two men no older than herself standing at the door, waiting for her to let them in. They counted the choice cards to make sure they were all there and checked with her that she had indeed chosen the *merbau*.

"That's a good one," the man with the gentle voice told her. "Not many of those these days. Since we've upgraded to Climate Control at the Back Yard, more and more are choosing trees native to the Americas, like fir and maple. It's nice to see someone going local every now and again."

They proceeded to cover her papa in a white cloth and carried him onto the roller-stretcher that was just outside her home.

"We'll be laying him into the sapling pod of your choice tomorrow and burying it the day after. You should give it a week or two before visiting the Back Yard, if you so wish."

The two men disappeared with her papa into the escalator. She closed her eyes, watching their movements through her mind's eye. She saw them zipping down sixty-two stories in that small, confined space. She saw them putting her papa, wrapped in that innocent white cloth, onto the back of their Transporter before folding the stretcher and loading it in too. She could even vaguely hear the whir of the engine and splash of water as the Transporter sped away, creating gentle waves and drawing a line in the sea from her apartment to the Tower of Eternity Pods: Where Memories Lie.

* * *

Mariska parked her rented Transporter and turned off the engine. The silence of the city that she had grown accustomed to was replaced now by a constant low-pitched hum, almost like a buzzing sound. It should have annoyed her but, strangely enough, the hum helped calm her down.

She took off her shoes and lined them up neatly before stepping off and grounding herself. The earth was cool, a little moist, and shifted ever so slightly under the weight of her body. She wiggled her toes, allowing the sensations to flow from the soles of her feet right to her heart. Then, feeling ready, she walked toward the arched entranceway of the Back Yard.

The earth underneath her was uneven, so different from the perfectly flat floors that they had everywhere in the city. It made her feel clumsy, almost as if she could easily lose her balance just taking another step. Yet humans are nothing if not extremely adaptable. By the time Mariska reached the large boulder by the archway, she could not recall what it was like to wear shoes on a concrete floor.

There were words carved into the boulder. They were so worn from being under constant rain and shine that it took Mariska a good moment before she could make them out.

Memories Lie Beyond
Pergunungan Titiwangsa, Tanah Air

Mariska recalled from a history class that the Titiwangsa mountain range was also known as the "backbone of the Malay Peninsula" a long time ago. This was before the sea levels rose so drastically that the mountains became islands separated from the mainland. This was before Malaysia, her ancestral country, formed a union of convenience with Singapore and Indonesia, its two neighboring countries. This union allowed them to share resources and prevent each of them from shrinking into ruin and oblivion.

Tanah Air was a compound word each of the countries shared in their respective native languages. It meant the homeland: the place you were born, the place you pledged allegiance to, and where you would finally lay to rest. It was also a quirky coincidence that the individual words translated to mean Land and Water.

Mariska gingerly made her way under the archway into the Back Yard. Immediately, the air around her took on a different aura, shimmering around her as she moved inward. The air felt lighter, drier, cooler one moment, then heavier, wetter, warmer the next. She held out her arm so that her fingers could graze, just barely, the barks of the trees that surrounded her. Trees of all types, all ages. Trees as far as her eyes could see.

And then she heard it. The voices. The spirits. Softly at first, but gradually taking up so much space that the low hum of the forest simply faded into the background.

The first time Mariska had heard the voices was when she was ten years old. Her mama had come home one day, excited about what she had heard from her friends at the Writers' Club. They had talked about a new medium who had holed herself up in the Stone Caves, and Mariska's mama was curious.

Mariska's papa was not as keen.

"You know as much as I do that there's no science to what these mediums are supposedly able to do," he argued. "We should be looking back to technology to propel us forward. Machines! Artificial intelligence! Things you can see and touch and program! All this hocus-pocus, spirits-in-the-air thing is just, well, nonsense."

Mariska's mama hushed him. "There's so much more to technology and advancement than robots," she said, and that was the end of it. They were going.

The Stone Caves were not too far from where they lived. It took them an hour on her papa's work Transporter, and soon they were parked by the long jetty. Mariska had looked up at the Stone Caves in awe, astonished to see such a majestic formation of rocks and greenery towering over her. Even more startling was the flight of stairs they had to climb to get to the entrance of the Stone Caves.

Mariska had never seen more than ten continuous steps in her life, so she made sure to count as they went up. Eighty-four to the top. There were more inside, leading to the middle of the cave where sunlight somehow found an opening amidst the rock formations and its surrounding trees to shine onto the roof of a small temple.

Mariska followed behind her mama as they quickly made their way toward the temple. Her eyes darted around, looking at the various statues of women in curious dresses staring back at her.

Some of them looked like they were frozen in dance. Mariska wondered if they had once been unfrozen, and if they had enjoyed themselves then.

Then suddenly she heard whispers in the air. Mariska paused and stared hard at the carved figures to see if they were in fact humans posing as statues, but none of them flinched. The whispers became louder the nearer she got to the temple, and soon they were tangible voices that took up space in her mind. She didn't even hear her papa coming up to her until he physically bent down to tug on her hand.

"Come on, Mari," her papa said. "Let's get going."

The medium was seated cross-legged on a small pillow in the middle of the temple. She had a kind face and was dressed in a long, beige-colored robe so different from the colorful dresses on the dancing figures. Mariska's mama walked up to the empty pillow in front of the medium and sat down facing her. They both closed their eyes, and everyone around them hushed.

For Mariska, this silence simply fueled the voices. They were now so loud they were practically echoing off the walls of the cave. She tried covering her ears, but the voices just penetrated straight into her. It was terrifying. She grabbed on to her papa's pant leg and held on for dear life, afraid of what might happen if she let go.

Just then, one of the voices rang louder and clearer than all the others, so clear that it shocked her. She was confused until she realized that the medium was saying the exact words that she could hear in her head.

Minah? Minah. It's Mama, can you hear me?

Mariska's heart skipped a beat. This stranger was calling out her mama's name. Minah's head snapped up and her eyes flew open, initial disbelief quickly melting into something between relief and heartache.

"Mama," Minah called out. "Minah is here, Minah can hear you. Can you hear me?"

The medium answered, but for Mariska, it was like having double hearing. Everything the medium was saying, Mariska could hear in her head, too.

Yes, Minah. I can hear you very clearly. Oh, I have missed you.

That was the only time Mariska had ever seen her mama weep.

Mariska tried to focus now, willing herself to add filter after mental filter, sifting through the spirits swimming around her to locate the one voice she was looking for. She made her way deeper and deeper into the Back Yard, and then she realized that the trees in these parts were smaller and shorter. Younger.

Mariska quickened her steps. Younger trees meant only one thing: these Eternal Pods had been buried more recently than the ones by the archway.

She was breathing heavily when she finally reached the valley. She knew the Back Yard extended far beyond the green hills in front of her, but right now, she had gotten to where she wanted to be. This was where the youngest saplings were.

Mariska looked around, silently chastising herself for choosing a tree that didn't have any uniquely identifiable features. Maybe the people who chose fir or maple knew what they were doing.

She willed herself to calm down. She waited, keeping still as she allowed the spirits to overwhelm her senses. She closed her eyes and focused inward, searching and searching for something to lead her to where she needed to go.

It came as a soft whisper, then disappeared amidst the other spirits. Mariska gasped, and in that moment, she understood completely how her mama must have felt all those years ago at the Stone Caves. The dull throbbing Mariska had carried in her heart the past two weeks lifted ever so slightly, and then turned into a sharp, pulsating pain that reached every inch of her body.

Mariska drew in a sharp breath. The cool air stung her lungs, but it also cleared the fog in her head. Suddenly, she had clarity. She didn't need to search anymore—she knew exactly where it was. And the nearer she got to it, the stronger that spirit's voice became. It was humming "Delta Dawn," the only song her papa knew to sing to her when she was younger.

He was humming this song that day, too, as he went about the kitchen preparing dinner for the three of them. Mariska had been helping him, picking the chives from their Plot Pot on the balcony while he cooked the water spinach and pounded the chili. The clock then made a beep, and Mariska turned to look at the door expectantly. Her mama always came home at the same time. Every day, without fail.

Every day, except that day.

They found out later that Mariska's mama had been involved in a three-way Transporter crash and was one of the four who had drowned as a result. Mariska had begged her papa to keep Mama whole, to let her have an Eternal Pod so that they could go visit. She pleaded, she threw tantrums, she even threatened to never talk to him again, but her papa would not budge.

"But I want to hear her voice again," Mariska had said to her papa. "If you burn her, what happens to her spirit? Where will it go? How will I get to speak to her again?"

"Mariska." Her papa never called her Mariska. "I don't want to listen to this nonsense anymore." Finally, it was the sadness she saw in his eyes that swayed and silenced her. It was a sadness that never left him, and he never sang "Delta Dawn" again.

The humming stopped as Mariska put her fingertips on one of the small branches of the *merbau* sapling. There was a moment of absolute silence. The spirits faded into each other and the forest crickets froze.

Mari?

Mariska hadn't realized she had been holding her breath. She opened her mouth and tears just came tumbling down her cheeks. She tried to call out to her papa, but her breath could hardly catch up with her accelerating heartbeat. She wanted to calm down, but she couldn't find her center.

So, she let go. And she wept like she had never wept before.

When Mariska finally found her voice, it was hoarse and nasally. "Papa," she whispered. "Papa, can you hear me?"

Mari?

"Papa," Mariska tried again, louder. "Papa, can you hear me?"

He could not.

Mariska looked down from the top of the stairs, then at the faded paint on the top stair. Two hundred and seventy-two. She had counted them this time, too. Eighty-two was a far way off from 272.

She made her way to the temple in the middle of the cave. The dancing figures had been given a fresh coat of paint and looked like they were having the time of their lives. There was a short queue in front of the temple this time. The medium had gained popularity as the people became more "spiritually attuned." It was all the rage now.

The spirits around Mariska were more varied than she remembered. Many of them spoke in a language Mariska could not decipher, but she understood the underlying feeling each of them had. They were spirits of longing, of memory, of a history and a past that they could not let go.

When it was Mariska's turn, she sat on the pillow in front of the medium the way she remembered her mama did. The medium still wore the same long, beige-colored robe, but there were now lines around the sides of her eyes, and her hair had taken a dignified shade of gray. She looked at Mariska for a moment before a light of recognition came over her face.

"I know you," the medium said. "You came once before, and I knew you then, as I know you now."

Mariska remained silent. In her head, she was replaying a conversation she had with her mama after their first visit here to the Stone Caves.

"I heard voices today, Mama," Mariska had said as her mama tucked her in for bedtime. "At the temple, I heard so many voices."

Her mama was startled. "Voices?" she asked.

"Yes, so many voices. All around me. Even the one you talked to."

"Oh, Mari," her mama said softly. "Those are spirits. They belong to the dead, their memories, and our memories of them."

"Did you hear them too?"

"No, I couldn't. Not everyone can hear them. That's why we had to visit the nice lady at the temple today. Because she can hear them too, like you."

"I tried to tell Papa about the voices. He didn't believe me."

Mariska's mama stroked her hair and planted a gentle kiss on her forehead. "It's okay, Mari. I believe you. And I'm sure Papa believes you too. He just doesn't understand yet. He will one day."

"You promise?"

"I promise. As long as you don't give up, he will understand one day."

"You want to be able to speak to them," the medium was saying to her now.

Mariska gave her a small nod, but her movement was so slight, she was worried the medium hadn't caught it. "Yes," Mariska answered out loud, her voice cracking.

The medium smiled, and Mariska thought that she looked just as kind as she did those many years ago.

"You already can," she said. "You just need to listen. Be patient. Be there."

The medium reached out and held both of Mariska's hands. "Don't give up. Don't give up."

Mariska felt her eyes welling up with tears. She pulled herself away from the medium's gaze and hurried to her feet. Mumbling a soft thank-you, she bolted out of the temple and down the stairs until she got to the jetty.

The medium had been soft and gentle when she held Mariska's hands, yet her touch had also sent a huge jolt through her body. It reminded her of how she had felt when she put her fingertips on her papa's Eternal Pod sapling, like she was hit by lightning and everything just fell away. The clarity of the moment was so pure and so brief, it scared her that she might never have it again.

After that, Mariska went to the Back Yard every single day. Every day she parked her Transporter, took off her shoes, and grounded herself on the soil. She stood there looking at the trees towering above her, listening to the sounds of the crickets mixed with the voices of the spirits, and she found herself rooted to where she was.

Some days she made it as far as the archway. But that was the extent of it. Mariska heard the spirits and felt an uncertainty creep into her heart.

The trees in the Back Yard grew and grew, as did Mariska's fear, until one day she simply stopped going.

There were no spirits in the city. No voices to grip at her heart and tie her to her memories. In the concrete jungle of Towers and Apartments rising solidly from water, Mariska slowly grew into a practical woman. She had a Memory Plaque made for her papa, just like the one her papa had made for her mama. She placed it next to her mama's Memory Plaque on the shelf in her room. She gave them each a minute of her mornings before leaving for work, and a minute of her nights before tucking herself in for bedtime.

Mariska learned the words to "Delta Dawn." She sang them every time she was in the kitchen, just like her papa did. Sometimes, she felt her papa's voice coming back to her, but every time it disappeared before she could grab on to it, and her papa's voice seemed lost to her forever.

Every once in a long while, she found herself remembering that feeling of clarity she had when she was standing in front of her papa's Eternal Pod. She wondered how much bigger the Back

Yard was. She wondered how tall the *merbau* tree was now. She wondered if her papa liked it, this final resting place that she had chosen for him.

She wondered if he was still singing "Delta Dawn."

WHEN IT'S TIME TO HARVEST

Renan Bernardo

I SAY TORRE VERDE VERTICAL FARM IS OUR MARRIAGE. IT'S A META-phor, of course. Juvenal says it's nothing like that. I rebuke saying the farm has been our home for the past forty years, and it's where we met for the first time and plucked our first lettuces from a growth gutter to make a salad for dinner. Juvenal insists that the farm—our farm—is just the means to an end, a collection of processes to feed a community of 300,000 souls. To which I reply that our marriage is also a means to an end, and the end is love. Our discussion usually ends when he says I suffer from GMTFS (Getting Metaphors Too Far Syndrome).

But, oh boy. Lately, I truly fear that instead of our marriage, Torre Verde might be our divorce.

Juvenal wants to retire. I want to too, only not now. I'm seventy-eight, he's seventy-nine, so he has a point.

"We're turnips far too ripe in here, Nádia." He sometimes utters a silly metaphor to provoke me—and make me laugh. (Sometimes we're potatoes, and when he's in a bad mood we're garlic.) His voice didn't change so much since he was a forty-year-old Black man with a degree in agricultural engineering and a bunch of friends with not enough food. Both of us didn't change much, actually. We're the same farmers we were then, eager to help the Tijuca community and happy to share the knowledge with other vertical farms around Rio de Janeiro. We share a set of completely human aches—backs and knees mostly—and have a vexatious tendency to forget new names and doze off when we're too still. Okay, maybe we did change a bit. But our farm—our marriage—is still too far from being a self-sustainable miracle for Juve to think about retirement.

The pen slips from my hand onto my lap. Again. No textbook writing when you stray yourself in thoughts about metaphors and retirement. I sigh and close the manuscript, a tan, bulky notebook, one of many Juvenal found in our building's cellar in a time when the water level was half a meter lower. He says I befuddle him with my simultaneous love for high-tech farming techniques and wrinkled, old-fashioned notebooks. I ask why he's calling himself a notebook. He walks away grunting, but I've been his wife for long enough to recognize a peal of muffled laughter.

I put the book on the night table beside my chair and touch my watch to call four pollinators. After a few seconds, they buzz down from the corridor's window. I stand and try to ignore the strain on my back, extending my palm up. The bees land on it, equidistant from one another. My nose isn't the same as it was back in my green days, but I can still feel the slight scent of strawberries and rosemary soddened in the bees.

I insert the four of them into a recharging station, and type an ID and a location into it.

"Kids, go fetch Juvenal's gift," I whisper, typing to release them. They quickly buzz out of the window.

Truth is, I'm sad we're tight in this bind. Juvenal needs rest, we need rest. It's been ten years that we've been looking at Isle of Forever Elderly Society, sited on an island off the coast of Rio de Janeiro. Self-sustaining auto-farms, recycling huts, self-sufficient energy generated through solar arrays and tidal lagoons . . . I love that place, yeah, but not as much as Juvenal does. For me it's like a pistachio ice cream; for him, it's a pistachio ice cream with chocolate drops and the promise of a flawless life. It's all he wants lately—not the ice cream, but the community. It's what he thinks—reasonably—both of us deserve after building and improving Torre Verde to the point of eliminating food scarcity in the Tijuca region.

The bees buzz back through the window, slower this time, bringing my pad, one tiny mini-drone on each vertex of it. I'd left it in the germination room, and they fetched it for me. After seventy, it's fairly sensible to use pollinators to fetch stuff for you. I turn on the pad and check the boat tickets. It's a five-hour boat journey underneath the scorching heat through the watery floodstreets of Rio out into the open sea and toward the Isle of Forever. But it's often worth the time—and Juvenal deserves to spend some time in his dream place after all the fights we've been having lately.

I leave my quarters and pace to the elevator and into the aeroponic level. Juvenal is talking with Julia, our trainee. The first thing that hits me is the pervasive scent of cabbage and chard coming from the growth towers. The second thing is the frown that sprouts across Juvenal's forehead when he makes eye contact with me. He quickly turns back to Julia, childishly avoiding my presence.

"The misters in this sector didn't spray the solution yesterday," Juvenal says, gaze fixed on Julia. He's wearing his usual blue dress shirt and khaki pants. His control pad—which he uses to play games and keep up with all the farm's statuses—hangs from his belt.

"We rarely have issues like that these days," Juvenal says, peeking closely at a tower of cabbages. Some of them are already dry, senescing under the lack of proper mist. "This often means a cascade of issues, Ju."

"I agree," Julia says. She's a twenty-eight-year-old agricultural engineer with a quaint and annoying way of quickly learning and solving everything she sets her mind to. She's the best we have. If Torre Verde is our marriage, the wedding vows are Julia. I'd also say she's the glue that keeps the farm intact in a healing, crumbly city. (Sorry, GMTFS manifesting itself). I keep looking at both of them with the pad in my hand as if I'm in a waiting room in my own farm—my own *home*. Clearly Juvenal is dawdling on purpose.

"The harvesting bots ignored this tower," Julia says, "and didn't perform the crop on the scheduled time because the mists didn't spray properly. And if the mists didn't spray properly, most likely nutripacks are missing from this section's nozzles."

I see a glint on Juvenal's eyes when the ceiling changes its lighting config. I'm sure he already connected all the dots in his mind. His sole purpose now is dawdling. I put my hands akimbo to show it's clear I know his strategies.

"And if there are nutripacks missing . . ." he says.

A flock of pollinators buzz across the corridor. Somewhere nearby, a harvesting bot is carefully selecting chards, its manipulators whirring softly.

Julia shrugs. "If there are nutripacks missing, then the swap drones didn't replace them correctly, which would make me believe packs are missing in the storage. But there isn't because I checked the system, so . . ."

Juvenal finally makes eye contact with me.

"I'm sorry . . ." I sigh, raising both hands. "I grabbed one of the packs and didn't update the system."

"Why would you remove a nutripack from the storage?" Juvenal says, and he knows the answer. I seethe, wanting to storm off and get back to our quarters to delete the damned ticket from the pad.

"I'm writing a chapter about them right now. I needed one for reference." I have no reason to justify my actions inside my farm to my husband/business partner/co-farmer. I only give him an explanation because Julia is there, and if she's our wedding vows, then I want to remain true to them. Damn, GMTFS.

"If you remove a pack from the storage without—"

"I know, right?" I raise a hand before he goes on. If there's one thing my old Juvenal hates it's human intervention in automated processes—exactly what removing a nutripack from the storage without updating the system is. "Can we talk?"

Juvenal nods, conscious I delivered him that pyrrhic victory. Julia beams an awkward smile and moves away. She's been with us for almost five years now, but she's still careful to tread the grounds of our relationship. She can tell us straight to our faces that we did something dumb or wasted some resource by meddling with the wrong part of the farm system. But she never intrudes in her bosses' bitter love. Sometimes I wish she did, though. Young folks are great problem-solvers.

When Julia is out of hearing distance, Juvenal kisses the tip of my nose. I kiss his. Yeah, we might be hating each other for the time being, but some rituals die hard. I brush off a tiny leaf from Juvenal's thinning hair. My throat is a bit sore. I grab the pad from my dress pocket and turn it to him.

He puts on his reading glasses.

"It's been two years we don't go . . ." I say.

He frowns at the pad, and for a while the only noise is the occasional pollinator buzz and the clockwork spraying of the mists coming from the racks' nozzles.

Juvenal shakes his head.

For the first time in almost fifty years of marriage, he's refusing one of my presents. I've got some violent lurches in my life: when my mother vanished when the water levels rose in Rio; when big corporations were still a thing, and one of them sent private troops to invade our building; when we wasted a whole month of crops with the wrong experimentation. But I have to confess that gift refusal hurts the most. Maybe it's only perspective, or maybe it's because we've been tautening our relationship as never before and it feels like pulling one's hair. Perhaps it's just because I didn't sleep well. But, oh boy, it hurts.

"I'm sorry, *amor.*" He notices how I feel. "Look at me. I'm shriveled, my leg's a mess, my back seems about to crack at any time. Next time I go to the Isle, I want it to be for good."

"We can't leave the farm, Juve," I stutter, knowing that's exactly the source of our quarrel.

"Your use of 'leave' means we can't stop working here," he says, taking off his glasses and folding them into his pocket. A cue he's done talking. "One day, 'can't leave' will just mean we're physically unable to travel."

"We're not fragile cabbage leaves, Juve." I snort.

"We're not sturdy growth racks, either." He doesn't find my comment funny, though.

I admit Torre Verde is extremely automated. But Juvenal thinks it's 100 percent automated. It is not. We still need Julia—she's a manager, an engineer, and a technician. She's the only one, fine. In the past, we had eighty people working full-time on the farm, and now we only need her as an integral part of it. Still, she's a human being—i.e., not fully automated. Apart from her, we occasionally hire and volunteer a few other people to coordinate cargo and distribution in the docks outside, and a few security muscles from the community to keep an eye on the building.

And it needs *us*—call us the Founding Couple, whatever. It needs me. I've been writing a highly comprehensive book, so future generations can learn and imitate what we do here, so other farms around Rio, Brazil, and the world can have a detailed manual of how to erect a self-sustainable, quasi-automated farm. It needs Juvenal, too. Between the two of us, he's the one with the mind filled with technical data, processes, model numbers, logs, history, and other stuff that I doubt even our systems have. Of course, lately he's been telling it all to Julia and typing it all into our data storage. He wants to make a point. Juve loves to make points. He thinks I don't see it, but he aims to make himself dispensable. He wants to prove to me that the farm doesn't need us anymore like teenagers using faulty arguments to prove they don't need to live with their parents.

I sigh. I've been drifting too much. The notebook where I'm drafting the book is open on the table before me, and I lost track of time. I set the pen aside and rub my forehead.

Chapter XXII: How the Torre Verde Pollinators Work (Part 2).

My favorite subject, and yet I can't drip a single word onto the page. I inhale the musty air of the hydroponics sector. I'm alone in one of the modules, sitting by a table I use exclusively for writing. The farm has some of these quiet spots I made for myself over the years. It's often in a corner out of the bots' algorithm paths. The occasional buzz of a pollinator and the distant warble of (almost) perfect synchronous working bots are the only sounds nearby. One day, years ago, I thought about what paradise could look like if it existed. I could go with either a solitary beach or a lush mountainside, but in either case, it'd have to have a spot like this one.

I pick up the pen and start writing. The ink's nearly running out.

> *As seen in the previous chapter, pollinators are equipped with nano-sensors capable of detecting when flowers are ready for pollination. Their tiny eyes and ultra-sensitive manipulators can distinguish the light greenish-yellow hues of anthers readying for pollination [see chapter XXI] and the way petals develop in the flowers. Some of them, those I like to call Queen Bees, are even set up to adjust the humidity and the temperature of an environment through signals sent to the respective floor's central control [see chapter XVI]. This pollinating system is self-sustainable and works with almost no human intervention, the exceptions being*

I stop.

It's not self-sustainable while it needs flesh hands! If a lot of bees malfunction at the same time, we'd need to purchase or fabricate new ones. Also, their stations don't come out of thin air like Juvenal would love to think; once in a while Julia has to cross the floodstreets to get new stations. It's not common, fine, but it happens. In all the flow diagrams of the farm, scattered amidst the blocks and arrows crisscrossing throughout components, there's always the tiny icon of a bald-headed, eyeless stick figure representing a human interaction. And does Juve want me to spend the rest of my life in a beachside dwelling while our farm—our marriage—crumbles, and hunger becomes once again a problem in the community? Yes, he does! And no matter how I outline the details and show him how we're still needed, no matter how much I love that hapless wise man, he still fails to see Torre Verde *is* us.

And here he comes. Peace: disturbed.

"Hey," he says, grunting and pulling the chair across the table from me. I know he wants to parley, and I know he'll try to muddle it with prior chitchat. It's his way of setting the mood. "The system changed the light uptake for the terraces' cilantro crops to compensate for this week's weather."

"Hmm . . ." I don't take my eyes off the notebook. My hands grip the pen tightly as if I'm able to escape from the conversation using it. Juvenal brings into the place his cologne's bergamot fragrance with hints of something else.

"This week has been darker than usual."

"Oh, I know . . ." I say, nodding, biting my lips, still not wanting to make eye contact. "A lot darker indeed."

"I'm speaking of the cloudy weather."

"That too." I nod.

Juvenal stretches his head to look at what I'm writing. I turn the notebook so he can read.

"I'm not wearing my reading glasses," he says.

"Pollinators, part two."

"Your favorite." There's a smile on his lips, a faint but tender line, barely leaving the neutral ground. He rubs his index finger lightly on the corner of the page and the feeble ink smears on his skin. "Ink . . ."

"What about it?" I almost roar.

He shakes his head. "There's a—"

"Make your point, Juvenal. You're always full of points to make. You're almost a scoreboard."

He frowns. "GMTFS."

I bite my lips but instead of rebuking him, all that comes out of my mouth is a muffled laugh.

"I was just going to ask you why you insist on these old notebooks," Juvenal says. "I gave you a WritePadXS 6.5 last year, and you barely even use it."

"Oh, I love that thing," I say. "But I prefer to write fiction on it. All my reasoning and logic for this book about Torre Verde works better when I'm spilling it out on paper."

"Speaking of which . . ." Juvenal taps his finger on my notebook.

Here comes his point. "Need to read some new story you've been writing."

No, it doesn't. But I'm angry anyway.

"You shouldn't complain if I decide not to use your gift. You refused mine."

His mouth hangs open. Okay, I thought *he* was going to be the one to verge our conversation toward awkwardness. I feel bad for an instant, wanting to prune away my words.

"It's rain and flood season . . ." he says. Now he's avoiding my gaze. I don't blame him. Perhaps he's just there to chitchat after all, and I'm the one provoking. "You know how tiresome the trip across the floodstreets is. And you want me to go to the Isle during hard weather so I remain tucked inside our cottage. It's almost like—"

"What? That the community is tedious enough to make you never want to come back there and instead stay here forever?"

Juvenal shrugs and his shoulders slump.

I pinch my lips, fidgeting with the notebook's hinge. "I bought the ticket with the option to change the dates if you wanted to."

"We're talking retirement for ten years, Nádia." He shows me both his palms. They're wrinkled with two arthritis-crooked fingers. I glance down at my hands resting upon the table. "Ten years."

"And you think this farm will resist without us? It might endure for a few months, maybe a year, but then? Do you think Julia knows everything about this place?"

"Well, she certainly knows a lot more than I did at her age."

"That's why I'm writing this." I pull the book back to me. "When this is done, and we have consistent information about everything we lived here . . . when I lay down all we created and you want to easily give away, then we can . . . retire." The last word feels bulky in my mouth.

"You said this to me before in a kind of vague way, but now I need to ask: Is this a promise? When you finish the book . . ."

"And publish it . . ."

"And publish it . . ." The lines around his cheeks are severe. I think of dehydrated collard greens. "Then we'll retire in the community and leave Julia as a permanent manager of this place?"

I say nothing. A promise is as strong as planting the seeds on a growth rack with the certainty that with proper lighting, the right nutrients, and a rigid schedule they would develop into a beautiful and fragrant set of purple chives.

"It is," I finally say, dry throat and all.

Juvenal beams the kind of smile I don't see often. It's not the smile of someone who won an argument, but of a person finding out flowers don't need to grow on the soil after all. He stands and carefully walks to my side of the table. I raise my head and stretch to kiss his lips. That "something else" that goes along with his cologne is a kind of sylvan, restful scent, something I'd associate with new families sprouting up in a beachside community. He grips my hand and leaves, still smiling.

I thicken the word "exceptions" on the text. But the ink is gone.

I take out a mobile recharging station from my pocket and set it to invoke two bees. I'm going to need a new pen.

Later that night, when Juvenal's already snoring his dreams away in our quarters, I decide the book will need at least two more chapters.

One thing I always wanted and never could get is an oil lamp. No matter how hard I scoured the floodstreets of Rio, I never found a good, old-fashioned oil lamp, something that screamed past and bucolic. The recessed and grow lights of the farm are always too businesslike-white for my tastes. I ended up writing under candlelight, and later, under pollinator light. Many of them are more like fireflies than bees, emanating adjustable lights from their spiracles that are often used to control the light uptake in some sectors. I arrange them across my studio to bathe me in what I call fake lamplight. If anything, inspiration comes easier.

Chapter XXIV: Maximizing Crop Output.

It's 3 a.m. and that's all I've written since 11 p.m. The pollinators' constant buzz is almost comforting, disagreeing with my slightly cramped fingers gripping the pen and the disturbing thought that when I made Juve smile I felt a bit sadder.

Torre Verde is divided into thirty floors and four main sections: processing center and management, aeroponics, aquaponics, and hydroponics. In a practical sense, it's far more than that: there are the fast-turn crops and slow-turn crops floors, auto-chute systems for waste disposal, germination rooms, greenhouses, hundreds of decontamination airlocks, nurseries, control rooms, storage tanks, distribution centers, management floors, and a lot of other stuff that makes that single building feed an entire community of 300,000 souls. And inside each of those rooms, a set of complex, nontrivial processes and components, each of them deserving a chapter in my book. At least a subsection.

"It's gonna take a while," I tell the room, writing in small letters on the corner of the page. *Idea for 2 or 3 chapters: the human components of the farm.* I've been writing, drafting, sketching diagrams, making notes. I made a promise to the man I love. No matter how I think the farm needs us, I'll finish this damn book and fulfill that promise.

My watch vibrates with a notification. *Pollinators shortage in 13th floor; sector hydro-B3; rack 2818. Quantity: 3.* I grab the recharging station and configure three of my tiny lamplights to address that issue. But before I can finish it, the white, undeviating lights of the room turn on and blind me for a moment.

An alarm starts to blare.

The last time a level 5 health-related alarm blared in Torre Verde was after the accident that killed Rogério Assunção. Juvenal and I had been in the passionate/euphoric phase of our relationship, not only between ourselves, but between us and the farm, the employees, the resources we gathered from bankrupt companies, the terabytes of information regarding what would become Torre Verde, the boats that came and went day by day carrying tons of growth racks, tanks, rotating beds, computing clusters, bioplastic fences, and everything we needed to erect our "manna tower" in the middle of a Rio severely impacted by the rising of the sea. Rogério was a technician electrocuted by a design failure in one of the germination-room projects. After that day, we committed ourselves to proceed with Torre Verde's projects only after every employee's safety was ensured.

I boasted to this day, until that alarm sounded off and cut short my writing, that the last serious accident in Torre Verde happened almost forty years ago.

My mouth tastes funny as I walk the fastest I can to the elevator and into the hydroponics section of the fourteenth level. Juvenal is splayed on the floor surrounded by a puddle of water. A harvesting bot stands inert next to him, a water basin hanging skewed from its manipulators.

"Juve?" I say, but my voice is barely audible even though I already turned off the alarm.

I kneel before him, ignoring the strain on my knees. We're alone. Julia went home at 8 p.m. But that's not supposed to be an issue. That's our home, our marriage. We're always safe here, right? Nothing bad ever happens.

"Juve?" I repeat, brushing the hair from his forehead. His eyes are open and squinted. He seems to be making an effort to recognize me. At least there's no blood I can see.

"I slipped," Juve manages to mutter, which makes me laugh in relief. "Oh, my waist hurts, sweetie . . . that bot's not supposed to be here."

But it is. Probably replacing the water of a hydroponic reservoir, somehow forsaking its main algorithm since our current config doesn't allow this kind of maintenance after midnight.

"I'm going to take you to the med room." I lift his head. Something sticky coats my hand.

Oh.

There's the blood.

"Call Julia on the emergency line," I say to my watch. But Juve can't wait. I need to take him to the med room and all I can think of is how it was I who put that bot there.

"Hello? Nádia?" Julia's voice is a relief that lasts until Juvenal grunts. The spilled water is reddening. *It's supposed to be creating life, not taking it.*

"Juve fell." It's all I can say. Julia hangs up. She understands what's happening.

But I can't wait for her. I set the emergency protocols in my watch and put my mobile recharging station on the wet floor. Making an effort to navigate the exceedingly small station interface, I invoke all Torre Verde's pollinators.

Juve passes out. I whisper his name as if it somehow can wake him. I fear removing my hand from the back of his head. I fear even shifting my fingers one centimeter.

I close my eyes and all I see are Juvenal's arthritic hands opening before me. *Ten years.*

While the pollinators—*all* of them—gather themselves around my Juve and lift him from the ground by their minuscule legs, the guilt weighs on me.

Yes, I put that bot in Juve's path. I made him fall.

My thoughts fluster in the same kind of logical processing Julia uses to solve problems. A farm is all about timing. That harvesting bot is only there because something disrupted its schedule. Something like removing a nutripack from the storage, which then cascaded into a set of events that positioned that particular bot in that exact place to exchange a reservoir at the same time Juvenal was probably sleepless and taking a walk. Fate. Doom. Call it whatever you like. Unraveled by me, a bald-headed, eyeless stick figure intruding in the farm's automation. Unfurled by each pollinator I disrupt from the system. By each chapter I decide to add in my never-ending textbook.

As I see my Juve flying away from me, hovering above the racks we built up out of love and necessity, I realize the farm's never going to be the way I want it to be. The farm *is* us. And our future is incognito.

The boat waits at Dock No. 1, not coincidentally a revitalized version of the one that Juvenal, a team of thirty-five farmers, and I arrived on so many years ago to a decaying building, heads filled with projects of feeding everybody we could.

"Seven minutes to departure," Julia yells from the dock, wheeling Juve's last luggage.

I'm already aboard the boat, elbows propped on the gunwale. On other docks, cargo autoboats come and go, mere nodes in the food-distribution web. Some volunteers help us load crates onto the boats, but most docks already function with the cranebots I developed in almost another life.

"I had more stuff than I thought," Juve says, smiling at me. I lift my hand to wave. Under the *brigadeiro* sky, unmarred and unclouded, I can almost catch his happiness. Despite his limp, he has recovered well from the accident, but the crutch probably will be his companion until the end of his days, a reminder of how Torre Verde can't be our marriage.

But neither is it our divorce.

After a few minutes, everything is set up and Juve joins me on deck, glancing one last time at the tower where we erected our lives. I sense the aerobic aroma of hydroponics, gourds, strawberries, rosemaries, and the subtle bergamot of my Juve.

"Will you miss it?" Juve says.

"Not as much as I missed you when the hospital reprinted a couple of your joints." I straighten a tuft of his hair behind his ears and kiss the tip of his nose. My fingernails are still crusted with dirt from the greenhouse harvest I did a few hours before.

"But I'm bringing some of it with me." I show him my nails.

He bursts out laughing. "GMTFS, my love . . . GMTFS."

Later, when the boat leaves the ever-receding floodstreet waters and sets off toward the Isle of Forever Elderly Society, I leave Juve staring at the open sea and withdraw to the boat's cabin.

Two bees bring me my pen.

Prologue: How to know when it's time to harvest.

BROKEN FROM THE COLONY

Ada M. Patterson

THE CORAL COULD NO LONGER TELL HER APART. HER BREATHING had slowed and so had her body. She knew she was running out of footsteps. A decade of walking would do that to a girl like her. The sand could sometimes catch her heels, distracting her to memory. Getting lost in who she once was and forgetting what she was becoming. That's how the stillness found her. Surrendering to the glimmers of a life above the water. Her life before the water. Quiet. Alone. Broken whenever the current breezed through her, its chill seizing her neck and voiding her pores of plankton, algae, and grit. Cold enough to remember what real wind feels like. Standing at the peak of some hill—what was its name again? Farnham? Or was it Felicity? No, that's just what she called the feeling. The name didn't matter. What mattered was the breeze. The mournful sigh of the Atlantic washing over her, only ever heard in branch rattle and casuarina shivers. And she could hear them. Each green strand swept up in a thousand breaths of wind and all its loosest fruit dropping from the sky like an emptied nest of sea urchins. She was careful never to walk barefoot under casuarina trees. The unwary shock of their fruit under heel could feel like glass thrust into bone . . . like lionfish barbs . . . the thorns of a blowfish . . . stepping on the fangs of a reef—the wind! Remember the wind! She can't afford to drown herself in similes. She must remember the wind. The wind cutting through her shirt. Sharp enough to remember where her nipples were. Are. Not polyps. Nipples. The ones she grew on purpose. The ones that were hers even before the changes. The changes in her body and the changes in her world. She could no longer tell them apart. The wind picking through her hair like casuarina. The Atlantic sighing with her. Staring out over that hill without a name, everything could be her. And she could be . . .

The current broke through. It reached into her and she remembered. She remembered where she needed to go, and she could once again pluck out all those questions that waited for her. How many days had she lost? How many footsteps did she have left? How long had the stillness claimed her? How much of her was still there buried beneath the coral? Her polyps could choke from these kinds of questions. Better to let them be carried away on the leftover gust of currents. Better to just keep moving for as long as she could. As long as her mind could outgrip the coral. How much farther was it? She tried to look through the black thicket of salt water. Any soreness would be softened by her second eyelids. She stared because she needed to know where she was. She needed to remember. Her neck hissed like shoreline avalanches when she turned to face the nearest landmark. Once, a supermarket. Now, a ruin brained in coral. Elliptical stars bloomed throughout the darkness. A colony of hungry mouths to feed . . . She never wanted to be that—a colony. She wanted a family, sure, but not whatever this was. Rooted and bound to your species. Repeating and repeating an ideal body. An ideal mind. Not allowed to have your own thoughts. Never able to see further than the horizons of the colony. No, she always wanted more than this. More than this place. More from this place. The coral stared back at her like it knew these wants would all be in vain. Like it knew that all that would ever grow in these waters was colonies. Her feet slipped into roots. It had found her again.

* * *

"That's your son?"

With a little flirt in his smile, her father lapped up this bait thrown by the checkout clerk.

"My eldest." He let his daughter die in his mouth.

Floating her palm a little lower than the counter, the clerk patted the head of a ghost only she could see.

"I remember he did small so."

She never understood why the only changes people seemed to smile at were height and age. Grow tall, not wide—a rule she would need to outlive. Lest she hear some malicious auntie or some ugly-on-the-inside family friend proclaiming their disapproval, "Yuh get fat."

Never a surprise to them. Just a disappointment. That her body could grow so unruly and out of line. She couldn't understand why stepping out of line had to mean stepping into harm's way. Neither the checkout clerk nor her father could see the newfound softness of her shape, skin, and hair. Nor did they notice the tasty shiftings of her fat. Between her welling emotional depths and all that sweetlike-Demerara joy she was living, none of it could be registered. They just didn't know what to look for. Too busy remembering a child who wasn't there. Too preoccupied welcoming a man who would never arrive. And so of course they couldn't see the changes. The ones that mattered. The ones that would keep mattering.

She stayed silent. Just idled away the moment, fattening her strung-out backpack with groceries. A monotony of cans broken only by a few standout treasures. Saltfish. Hot pepper. Cucumber. Everything piling up, the mouth of her bag hung agape in horror. She lost herself in the wafting foulness of breadfruit, left behind from some acrid gully. It was still cupping a haunting of crushed ants, wet grass, and the far-off stink of freshly dead fieldmouse. But this was, she knew, the way to pick breadfruit. It should smell like it's rotting from the inside out. After all, what they call yelluh meat is just a ripening dressed in decay. When the flesh falls apart, sweet and off. Just like her. Yelluh meat—what both men and women searched for buried in her thighs. Something discoloured from race and so debased it didn't have a gender. All the most sumptuous changes had smelled like something dying. And something dying could taste like heaven. And they knew that, the men and women. So, they craved her. They craved her centipede-bite lips and her little coucou-scooped breasts. She was loose wet sand. Sticky where it mattered, but never fully graspable.

Locking the teeth of her backpack, she rushed ahead of her father. She needed to get away from the distracting scents of dead boys and breadfruit. She needed some air. They still hadn't noticed her, and on today of all days. Her sixth month on estrogen and they just couldn't see it. All that moved within her. And, in the beginning, maybe that was the point. To touch this change invisibly. To transform before their very eyes, hidden in plain sight. Each day, she'd let it melt into her. Let it drop below the surface. The ripples it would leave behind moved with the kind of slowness and subtlety that had kept her undetectable. She could hide herself in raindrops. And with each day, she would feel a little bit different. It could hardly be measured except for maybe that singing tingle in her nipples and a fresh clinginess from the grasp of her shirt. She felt a little bit softer and she walked with a little more rhythm—and she didn't think that was chemical. She just felt happier to hold her own narrative again. Lighter, now that her drowned life could find another kind of breath fluttering below the surface. Maybe it was chemical. A pill that let her breathe underwater. And for a while, that metaphor could be real enough to float on. To walk on land unscathed. Unscathed enough, at least. Disappearing when she needed to, deep into the body of a man who lived in the eyes of others. His skin would keep her warm, moist, and breathing. And she would do what she had to. She was not prepared to drown. Not here. Not like this.

Outside, the sun had no mercy to spare. Limestone and construction dust choked the air in white. The street was arid and thick with noise. No room for softness here. Jackhammers razed the ground to powder while minibuses feted down the road. Car horns screamed aimlessly to the sky as if God Himself would divert the traffic. Dorian was coming and he wasn't playing. His was the only name worth remembering. Everyone was bracing themselves with groceries. A hoard of plastic bags bursting with dry food and cans. People buying up all the provisions they could carry. You'd think the cans were filled with hurricane repellent. Out on the pavement in front of the supermarket, she stood in the middle of it all. This storm before the storm. Soaking it in, she let what little breeze there was tickle her hairy legs. From her washed-out, ashy denim shorts, a line of sweat painted itself down her inner thigh. Beads of terra-cotta skin poking through the moth-holes in her shirt, hoping to catch this excess of light.

She was staring off toward the entrance. Keeping guard of this precious moment where she could just stand in her body and not be seen otherwise. By her father or by anyone else for that matter. A plaster arch sheltered the doors. It was dressed without a soul in a sandy hue of magnolia. The whole building actually, except for its navy, orange logo. Altogether, it looked like someone who hated sunsets painting with their colors. It was meant to read simple and stylish. For the tourists, whose tastes were first to serve. The central supermarket for the resort district. What an eyesore. She recoiled. A magnolia storehouse heaving with burnt salmon bodies. She always wondered how they managed to get so red while still stinking of sunscreen. But this place wasn't for them today. No one could afford to think about tourist dollars when there was a hurricane to shop for. She lowered her eyes on those she called her people. The automatic doors opened and closed like a panicked heartbeat. Families pouring through with children hanging on each arm. They all firmly believed survival was something you bought in a store. The only belief more unshakable was thinking God was from this island. As far as they knew, His navel string was buried here and deep within every one of them. They could never accept that God had left with the British.

This is what she loved doing. Vanishing into the lives of other people. Her people. Taking a highbrow pity on them to avoid the reality that she and they were so painfully bonded and alike. She never really belonged in other ways. So, she loved them difficultly and from afar. Mostly with complaints and criticisms. She wanted more from them. For them. But she loved it. This game of pretend in moral superiority. Nestled in her judgments, she felt unseen and therefore invincible. She was never waiting for her father. No, she was savoring this joy untethered from looks that never knew how to read her. Spreading herself wide in the world in those seconds before his return. Bleeding out among all the noise, thinning into dust, burning with the sunlight, and drifting on the breeze. She knew how to be everything when nobody was looking.

* * *

A handful of polyps crumbled from her eyelids when she finally came to. All of her panicked for a second, trying to catch her breath too fast through every living pore. Which body was she in now? She patted herself down. No moth-eaten shirt. No denim shorts. Just rubbery brown skin oozing with curls and coral. Her memories could be dangerous. Fatal, even. And right now, she couldn't afford to be disembodied from the present. The past was underwater and she didn't want to drown in it. Not again. Turning her back on the coral colony, she kept moving. A little farther uphill and she would have made it. Keeping the distant past bubbled out of mind, she stayed with the road ahead and her life below the surface. The trouble brewing in her body could sometimes soften when she let the beauty of this world shine on her in wonder. And it was a resonant beauty. One that made real sense to her. Drowned, fragile, and in parts, ruined. But full of the promise of life. And life that lived together. An interconnectedness she couldn't easily remember. Surviving independently not beside but with each other. Rainbows of shrimp nursing anemones. Anemones protecting their tenants from harm. Coral and algae living in close quarters. Keeping each other alive. Caring for each other's bodies like we lived in each other's bodies. She always smiled when she saw this. It was all so foreign to what she remembered before Dorian. And she would smile harder knowing that life here lived everywhere. There were no empty enclosures. No annexed lands. The road was lined with sunken villas. Forever vacant in the past, now swarmed with coral and peopled by fish. Everything grew where it could. No permission needed. Just a fighting chance and a helping hand, fin, claw, tentacle, or polyp.

Villas started turning into the remains of chattel houses as she continued up the road. Trying to find the sun, she looked up to the surface ceiling above her. It was cloudy with sargassum. Forests of amber seaweed as thick as an eclipse. She could make out little pockets of sunlight whenever the clouds parted with the waves. The surface had always been restless, just as everything beneath it. She convinced herself that as long as it kept stirring, so would she. She didn't really have a choice. The restlessness had held her ever since that day. Like a dead body washed ashore from aimless days of drift, the news came running on the water. A Vincentian fishing boat spotted it. Rising from the sea, a mound of sand and limestone struggling to stay afloat. It wore a crown of dead black trees. A giant sea urchin. That's how the fishermen described it. The humble peak of Mount Hillaby, which was nothing more than a slope of dirt and bush, poking out of the water like a bobbing skull. All that was left of her island and she was determined to see it. She was born there and she would die there. Everyone else had died there. Those who found life below the surface—her and the other girls—they were never really living in the first place. Her

people had made sure of that. When the water came and left her
people for dead, she got stuck in the loop of a question:

"How do you grow up on an island without ever learning how
to swim?"

She asked it without judgment. It was something driven by a
child's curiosity. Knowing how to swim wouldn't have saved any
of them—she knew that, of course. Nobody could outswim a hurricane. Yet the question still troubled her. Every time there was a
drowning, the island would swell in grief. Local and tourist alike
had been claimed by the sea, but death never seemed to play fair
when it came to the lives of her people. From this, she reasoned
that death must be a tourist too. That, or a hotelier. She knew how
her people got here. It wasn't a secret for her generation. Ships
brought their ancestors in all kinds of chains but she didn't think
any more sense could be wrung from that journey. That is, any
sense that hadn't already been written to death. That hadn't written her people to death over and over and over again. Why would
she rub manchineel in her eye in the hope of understanding it?
And after all that senselessness, this little rock of horrors, trembling in the Atlantic, suddenly had to hurtle itself into a society.
That question again making her seasick: How do you grow up
on an island without learning how to swim? Its shadow mocked
her and her people. Why would property need to swim? Where
would it need to swim off to? She grew suspicious of the drops of
white in her that made these questions all too easy to imagine.
She feared her blood for what it could want if hers was not the

body to hold it. She tried to salvage something from the wreckage of that journey.

"Who the hell would want to swim after all that horror on the water?"

It still wasn't enough to soothe her. She couldn't leave her people stranded there like that.

She looked to what was left of all the chattel houses that used to hug the road too tightly. There was hardly anything there to remember them. All their wood had drifted. Waves of galvanised paling rusted into loss. Only foundations remained. Rows of concrete steps going nowhere fast. Portals of memory drowned in the sea. Some of the yards were haunted with statues and birdbaths. A mold of some nameless little white boy with a basin on his head. The same child cast in concrete and painted enamelwhite to live in every single yard on the island. She could see his pristine whiteness didn't last. He was encased in the blades of sea fans and an ooze of pink coral. Sea stars nested in his basin. Not a bird in sight. Just shoals of fish floating around, indifferent to this child's drowning. The question haunted her again. She knew how much love she had for the island. Only her people could rival her in that. But she never wanted to be stuck there or anywhere. She could never reconcile that there were those who didn't want or need to leave. Those who didn't need to swim. Where would they need to go if the land had everything they needed? That little rock could be enough for them. And this thought stirred her like a hurricane. She clenched her fist and teeth. All she wanted was to hold her little rock in her hands and know it was enough. She tightened around the memory and could feel it warming in her fist. But that rock and her people stared back at her ugly, ugly, ugly. There was no love grown for girls like her. A cold reminder that bloodied her hands with urchin thorns. She knew it would never be enough. Every day before Dorian, she had stepped off-island and into the water. She needed to float in everything that wasn't landlocked or left for dead. Every horizon was a possibility. Every black depth, a promise that stranded was not the only way to live.

And when Dorian came, the water stepped into her. They had broadcast the disappearance to the rest of the region. A whole island gone. No sign of survivors, which was true. Nobody made it out the same. They say the sea has no backdoor. But for girls like her, the sea was their backdoor. Girls growing soft with gills, pores, and polyps, just as they had grown otherwise. That little pill—that little piece of care—was one of the keys to their survival. Breath had been found underwater. As above, so below. Changing in the ways they needed to. And the sea—so choked with plastic—she changed too. Toxic microbeads. Hormonal plankton. Water in transition. Everything it held, changed. She knew what it was like to suffocate, both her and the sea. And so, she breathed what she could once the air began to thin. Oxygen depleted, estrogen on tap. A different kind of breath for a different kind of life for a different kind of girl. They were one inside each other, she and her—the sea and her. She and all the girls who made it through. A plural her of infinite pleasure. Everything wet was her. She oozed back into memory.

* * *

"Is funny." Keona's eyes landed on the horizon.

"What?"

"Girls like we"—they paused, lightly grazing the coral blooms budding on their brow—"always had to live 'pon the edges. Alone." They pointed out toward the horizon, showing her the way to where the island was missing.

The sea was quiet. It was wearing the embers of an evening's dying sun. Each mumbling wave collapsed on itself before it could rise, retreating back to the hem of its mother's skirt as if frightened of growing up. She could hear the pitter-patter of sandpipers zigzagging along the shoreline, their tiny feet leaving the lightest trail of fork prints. The twilight cooing of wood doves calmed everything in sight. It always sounded like a mourning song. Maybe they lost something too, she thought. The breeze was sighing all over, caught in the hands of almond branches and the netting thick of manchineel. Everything looked softer than it was. Pink and fuzzy. Even the wreckage looked more like an innocence of driftwood and less like death on its way out. Yes, the sea was quiet for the first time in months. It needed no words and no apology. Now, all this world wanted was to rest. She and the other survivors had been living in the shores and shallows of La Soufrière ever since the sea unbuttoned itself. Made up of lost coral girls and

Vincentians evacuated from the lowlands, after so much death had risen from the water, people didn't much care what you looked like, who you loved, or what bloomed on your body or between your legs. It was a village cathected in hardship and grief, and the most family she had ever known.

She was helping Keona nurture a fire. Everything they needed came floating on the water in salvageable debris. Crisis and redistribution—a hurricane promises both. A cast-iron pot burned black in the fire, its mouth gargling hot salt water with a plump clay bowl islanding its center. The pot lid, upside down, would catch all the vapor and drop it in the bowl. Freshwater for those in the encampment who needed it, for those who couldn't drink straight from the sea. Looking up from the fire, she rested her eyes on Keona. A bit older, their short, dark, woollen hair was blowing tiny smoke rings from each pore of their scalp. Their skin was a night sky on fire from all the heat that beaded their face with sweat. They were wearing an oversized turquoise button-up as a dress. Dirtied from life, it tried to swallow their body but couldn't stomach their thighs. Thick with a happiness of fat over muscle, they glowed greasy from the flames they were determined to keep alive.

"Look." They blinked away some sweat. She was always a little nervous whenever Keona began to speak. Their words sometimes had the power to encircle her like waves.

"All the edges closer now. Is only edges left back." She held her breath, letting their voice wash over her. Beneath her feet, the island receded. She tried to anchor herself, knowing Keona would never try to hurt her. Their words were difficult but she knew they would always be a gift. She weighted herself in it, dropping to the seafloor of Keona's offering. The edges grew closer and she let herself feel what that could mean. She could hear the village buzzing around her. People working to keep themselves alive. Doing this by keeping each other alive. A mixture of voices, once bodied with threatening differences. The luxury of fear scraped out like a coconut's heart. Dorian had come and pushed them all together. To here, of all places. A barely there village bowing meekly at the skirt of a volcano. Sardined by disaster, their worlds grew small and overlapped. There was nowhere to hide here. No need to hide.

Her breath returned, steady and grounded. Keona had felt her rolling their words around the mortar of her mind. They looked over her slowly, taking in this girl—this newfound sister—and all they shared together. They scanned the coral budding down the lengths of her arms. Each flower was ripe and supple. Hundreds of tiny amber lips pouring out of her. What were they becoming, she and Keona? Not quite coral, not quite human. But between wasn't where they were, either. Keona gave her a look of affirmation, letting their gaze hold the coral on their sister's body. She could feel what Keona was seeing, the blurry vision of herself becoming just a little clearer. She could feel herself feeling seen as an entirely new experience, one that could outswim any known horizon.

"You think they hear 'bout we?"

"Who?" Her brow furrowed.

"You know, them girls 'pon the other islands," Keona's words slipped their way in like high tide. Her mouth hung open trying to catch an answer. She was only just getting settled on this island. She hadn't had the space to think about other islands, let alone other girls. Keona's point had again unmoored her. Theirs was the island chosen to disappear completely in the roulette of seasonal disaster. Nowhere had stayed the same, but the other islands were still there. They had survived effacement. And there were still girls out there. Landlocked girls, stranded, trying to make life on the edges of other islands. Had anybody told them what had happened, what had changed?

"And what if they did?" she challenged Keona to soothe her.

"Well, think if it was you. What you would do?"

Keona wasn't easy at all. They let the challenge slip back into her hands like a glob of jellyfish. But she knew all too clearly what she would have done. If she knew she couldn't drown, she would have stepped straight into the water and never looked back. Safety at the surface was never something she could rely on. The safest space she had known was in the belly of the sea. But it was a safety bought with loneliness. Swimming out into the deep, she knew that no one could endanger her because she was the only one there. It could never be enough for her, of course, but now maybe it didn't have to be. The water's surface trembled in her mind, giddily breaking with all the possibilities. She could see them on the horizon, a sea of girls like her. Bodies both like and unlike hers, and the ocean was big enough to hold all of them. Lungs filling with seawater, new-growth corals breathing in their place, they could drop their shoulders, loosen their swinging hips, and let all that salt air untether them from harm. She loved that for those girls. She wanted all of it for them. And for her, too. She let her vision pool in her hands. Turning their backs on the surface, they would find it. A whole new world to breathe in.

* * *

The seaweed was beginning to thin above her and the water grew shallower and shallower. She could feel the sun burning through like holes gnawed out of a rusty tin roof. Its stinging woke her up. Her body knew it was almost time. She would soon become a colony. Beneath her, the road disintegrated into sand and mud. It was much saltier up here. It all looked so murky, except for the black wet roots that tentacled the ceiling. Everything felt unstable, slippery and dark, like she was crossing a dying mangrove. Maneuvering the brambling roots, she noted all the grief as she climbed toward the surface. Fruit trees bowed low, stripped of their bounty. Palms and pawpaw stalks swayed headless in the wheezing current. The ground beneath her, a skull of limestone razed of any and all memory. Like no blood had ever spilled here. Like no cane ever grew. Sunken out of place, everything lay damned. And with each step, the water turned hotter and greener. It was hard to move in this much heat. She could barely think. The mud was biting her heels and all her polyps screamed into the sun. Since she, the coral, and the water were bonded by the breath, she worried the surface was still no place for girls like her. It glittered right atop her head, trembling from its own ripples. She stared upward, frozen, as if the ceiling were going to collapse. As if the sky would drop a house on her for who and what she was becoming. For who she'd always been. A girl who swam too far out, now turning to come home. Light danced on her face and the gentlest pain fluttered across her, tingling any new corals that had begun to flower.

The shape of the island was pooling through the surface. Reading the ripples, there wasn't much to look at. It was scalped of anything she would have recognized. She could only make out some blackened spindly trees eeling into the sky. It did look like a sea urchin, she thought. Small, fragile, and protective of itself. Just trying its best to survive in a turbulent world. Beautiful to see and dangerous to touch. She wondered whether the island would let her hold it this time. Right beneath the surface, she continued to hesitate. She didn't know how to move and that wasn't because of the coral. The decision to resurface was pinning her in place. Nothing here was recognizably her island. She didn't know what she was returning to. Everything was new. It had just resurfaced. And she wasn't sure if she even had the right to demand so much from this place. She didn't even know if the island could remember her. She just kept looking, not sure what to make of it. This fragile little place flickering through the unsteady window to the surface. She watched as it trembled in the play of light and water. Over and over, it was dissolving, falling apart and coming back together, like it couldn't decide what it wanted to be. The island just kept changing.

THE CASE OF THE TURNED TIDE

Savitri Putu Horrigan

THE BOAT JOSTLED AND EVERYTHING WENT SIDEWAYS. I FLEW TO Mom's side, worried that her wheelchair would tip over and hurt her, but she had an iron grip on one of the many grab bars scattered throughout our boat home. The sound of things crashing around us quieted as the rocking abated, but my stomach was in knots from the suddenness of it.

"Was that an earthquake?" I asked. Mom shook her head, none the wiser.

"You stay here," I told her. "Let me just check that there's nothing sharp on the floor." Mom nodded, her eyes wide and hand still clutching at her chest. We have had fewer earthquakes since the Decree was passed, slashing public and private funding to the fossil fuel industry and redirecting that capital toward renewable energy solutions. It also implemented social programs to minimize and contain the effect of climate change on island nations like ours and funded humanitarian relief efforts for those left houseless from climate-related disasters. Mom grew up in that time where chaos abounded, the devastating impacts of earthquakes and tsunamis compounded by increased frequency, and widespread mitigation efforts seemed like nothing but a dream. She didn't talk about it much, but it was possible that shakes like this surfaced old memories of those times and any loved ones who might have suffered.

I made my way gingerly across the living room, picking up books and pillows to clear the path for Mom's wheelchair. I picked up a framed picture of my brother, Arjuna, and Dad in front of their apartment in town where they stayed while Mom and I had active cases. Ever since my apprenticeship in Mom's expanding detective business, this boat had become more of a home for me than the cramped space of our stifling-hot two-bedroom apartment.

Thankfully, boat living had conditioned us to leave our breakables in locked wooden cabinets. Unfortunately, one of those cabinets had burst open and shards of multicolored glass, clay, and ceramic pooled around it. I turned back toward Mom and said, "Don't come near the storage wall until I clear this up. We'll just have to use that bamboo set your friend gave us for the time being."

"Oh!" Mom called out, and the sharpness of her voice made me think it was out of pain.

"Mom! Are you okay?" I called back.

"My Barong statue! Something smashed it," she moaned. I used a brush to scoop up the broken kitchenware and locked the cabinet before jogging back to her.

"What happened?" I asked. She just stared at the barely recognizable pile of paint-chipped wood at her feet. The Barong was a mythical lion often placed in homes for protection. Only the statue's large eyes and wide, toothy mouth remained whole. I placed my hand on her shoulder. "I'm sorry, Mom. That really sucks."

Mom sighed and picked up the larger pieces. "I've had this since I was young. My parents gave it to me when I married your father." She sounded broken, but there was little I could do, and our clients were arriving soon.

"I'm sorry, Mom," I repeated. "Maybe we can find someone to fix it?" I scooped the pile onto a scarf and tied it up, storing it in a bag for safekeeping.

An hour later, our clients entered our living room and settled on the freshly cleaned couch. They were dressed immaculately in cotton slacks and blazers, and sustainable shoes made from seaweed and recycled plastic. One of the clients, Betty, had tan skin and sleek blond hair tucked into a side ponytail. The other, Arnold, had brown skin and curly dark hair that hung over his eyes. They looked around the small room, and I saw their eyes land on the government-issued Sea Debris Scooper that public and private boats were required to install for passive collection of microplastics and inorganic material. It gave off a gentle whirring sound that some found unpleasant but didn't bother Mom and me, who were just happy that we could benefit from it without having to break the bank. Betty and Arnold were representatives of Sea Debris, a Dutch company that created large-scale commercial environmental solutions.

"I see you have one of our best sellers," said Betty.

"And our saline-resistant solar panels," Arnold commented, craning his neck to better see the panels fastened to our upper deck.

"Yes," my mom said mildly. "Your products are a point of pride for us."

"Then you'll be pleased to learn that we have a new product coming out this summer," Betty replied. "A state-of-the-art technology for harnessing tidal power and wave energy for the masses. This will bring much-needed diversity to existing renewable energy infrastructure and reduce the chance of homes like yours being stranded at sea after a string of cloudy days."

"We've done extensive tests on our prototypes," Arnold added, "and are scheduled to deploy models this summer for major cities across the world. Your capital, Jakarta, will receive one as well."

"That sounds great," I said, excited about the major news but feeling confused about the direction this conversation was taking.

"Which is why we need your help," Betty said. "This technology is highly innovative and could drastically change the market for tidal energy. But just as we were about to ship the final blueprints to our partners, they went missing. Along with one of our engineers."

"We suspect that this engineer ran off with the blueprints and is planning to sell it to one of our competitors," Arnold continued. "If they patent our technology, it would be impossible to fight for proprietary rights, and the debt we've accrued from funding this research could destroy us."

I glanced at Mom and could tell we were wondering the same thing. How could a company that raked in millions each year from private and public partnerships possibly be in debt?

"Do you have any information on this engineer?" Mom asked.

Betty produced a tablet and swiped to unlock it. On its smooth surface a calm face framed by dark wavy curls peered back at me, their brown skin and brown eyes achingly familiar. They looked Indonesian, but I was not sure until I scanned the text below their picture and saw their country of origin and last place of residence: Jakarta. Their first name was recorded as "unknown," which was not uncommon due to the different naming structures of different countries. But aside from basic information on appearance, background, and length of employment at Sea Debris, the file revealed shockingly little.

"Is this everything?" Mom asked with an arched brow.

"Unfortunately, yes," Arnold replied. "Although Pertiwi worked with us for nearly ten years, she kept a low profile. When we interviewed her supervisors, they didn't have much to say other than noting her stringent work ethic. In fact, she never took time off, except once a year for something called Nyepi, which is . . . ah, some kind of local holiday from her hometown Jakarta," he said with a shrug.

Nyepi was a Balinese holiday. It shouldn't surprise me that they would mix up the traditions and customs of different islands, but my heart grew heavy with the knowledge that we were going to have to find and turn in someone from the same island as us.

"We can make do with this," Mom said, bringing me back to the conversation. She entered her code into the tablet so that Pertiwi's file could be uploaded to our virtual case management system with encryption for confidentiality. Mom discussed our payment policy with Betty and Arnold before leading them outside to our dock and promising to contact them frequently with updates.

We dove headfirst into the investigation, splitting up tasks like running Pertiwi's information through local record systems, scouring news articles and social media, and making inquiries to banjars across the island. Mom was insistent on reaching out to the banjars herself, as these community groups often acted like local government and had key, intimate insight into the goings-on of their towns and neighborhoods. Building trust with the banjars was easier to do if you spoke the local language, Basa Bali, instead of just the lingua franca, Bahasa Indonesia, which had been adopted for inter-island communication. Mom was fluent in both, while I could only speak the latter. That was just as well since I also had to tamp down a general feeling of unease about this case, and the best way to do that was through tedious tasks like navigating data systems and hashtags.

Hours later, our solar-powered lamps kicked on as the sun dipped below the horizon of gentle, lapping waves. None of the people we contacted had gotten back to us yet, but I did enjoy some of the posts that came up in my social media search. Searching for variations and combinations of different terms came up with lots of random posts and rabbit holes, but one of my favorites was by a local singer crooning an old ballad with the description "for Pertiwi" under the video. She looked to be about my age and had an amazing voice, strumming along on a guitar and wearing a white kebaya top with a frangipani flower tucked behind one ear. It looked like she had just come from temple, with the sun streaming through some banana trees behind her. Switching on Bluetooth, I played the song over from the beginning so Mom could enjoy it as well.

She hummed along for a bit, tapping her feet in time to the music. "This is nice," she said. "What song is this?"

"It's that old song that used to play on the radio a while back, remember? This singer tweaked it a little for an acoustic version, and I found it because she dedicated it to someone named Pertiwi," I said with a chuckle. We knew from our records search that there were hundreds of people with that name on this island.

Mom nodded then turned back to her work. A moment later, a small chime went off on someone's device and Mom scooted back from her table with a loud whoop. "We got a reply!" she said with excitement and turned around to flash me a broad grin. "Tomorrow we'll meet with Banjar Mimpi for lunch. They said they are willing to sit with us and hear our questions."

* * *

The next morning, we took an automated, zero-emissions hydro-gen train up north to a town named Mimpi. The open market was packing up, and activity on the streets had thinned as a result of residents and schoolchildren taking their lunches to some shaded retreat. It had been a while since we ventured into these parts, and I was not sure if the infrastructure here would be accessible for Mom. However, we were pleasantly surprised to find that most of the buildings surrounding the town center were equipped with railed rampways made from cork and recycled rubber tires. The roads were also well paved and spacious enough for Mom's elec-tric wheelchair, which is standard-issue and fully funded from the post-Decree People's Healthcare Plan. Its embedded gyroscope and spherical frame made from molded bamboo and reclaimed metal is phenomenal at keeping her upright on any terrain regard-less of slope, but does require smooth surfaces to operate on.

Mom led us toward a raised pavilion that was open to the elements but blissfully shaded from the sun in most parts. We removed our shoes before rolling up the ramp, ducking under a sign hung overhead that read "Banjar Mimpi," and were greeted with a burst of intoxicating aromas. We neared the table where food was being served, drawn to it like flies, and ogled the vast array of sumptuous dishes. Creamy coconut rice; spring rolls loaded with julienned veggies; crispy fried matchsticks of tem-peh tossed with peanuts in a sweet-and-spicy sauce; curried tofu and potatoes; chilled, spiced local veggies and seaweed; and my personal favorite, gado-gado. I zoomed in on the dish of crisp bean sprouts, green beans, chopped cabbage, tofu, and congealed steamed rice cakes slathered in heaping amounts of spicy peanut sauce, my mouth watering at the heavenly smell. But before I could grab a bowl, Mom grabbed my arm in a steel vice and leveled me with her most severe *don't-even-think-about-it* stare.

"My apologies," Mom said, and I belatedly realized that she had been talking to someone. A tall man in his sixties was standing next to her, his hair close-cropped and wispy white against mottled dark brown skin. He was dressed in a well-worn short-sleeved shirt with a sarong wrapped around his waist that featured a lovely batik pattern in burnt umber. "My daughter must have been distracted," Mom continued, giving me the side-eye. "This is Pak Surya, he is the head of the banjar for this town. He has graciously invited us to lunch with him and his husband, and then after we can ask any questions we have."

"It's very nice to meet you, Pak Surya," I said as my cheeks flamed with embarrassment. "You and your husband are very generous." Despite the hunger churning in my stomach, it was no excuse for my rudeness. He smirked knowingly and nodded toward the food, indicating that we should serve ourselves before joining him in the center of the pavilion.

We joined Pak Surya and his husband, Pak Jendra, on some faded but sturdy rattan chairs. As soon as they lifted a delicate handful of food to their mouths, I inhaled my gado-gado and sagged in delight at its comforting texture and flavor. My dad's version would always be my favorite, but I loved how spicy Pak Jendra's dish was and how the local veggies he had used were crisper and sweeter than the ones in our town. He'd also added small boiled rice-paddy snails that were delightfully chewy and combined well with the steamed rice cakes made from a red variety grown only in this region.

Pak Jendra grinned at me. "I'm glad you like my cooking," he said, leaning into his husband with affection. "You might already know that I source all of my food from this town and its surrounding area. This red rice is a source of pride for me, in particular."

"Many years ago," Pak Surya said, "we almost lost all our rice fields. If our crops weren't being ruined by scorching heat or flash floods, they were buried beneath landslides or ransacked by people fleeing sea-level towns and cities."

Pak Jendra's grin faded. "It was a struggle to feed ourselves during that time. But we realized that by adapting our existing subak irrigation systems to fit the changing needs of our fields we could mitigate at least some of the damage. We turned our temples into shelters for the houseless, who assisted our priests in measuring rain patterns so that we could predict the flow of water downhill and ensure that every rice paddy was equally fed. We banded together to advocate for policies in the Decree that now offer stronger protections for our land and resources. Over time, conditions improved and now we can rest knowing our grandchildren won't be hungry and that our cuisine can still be enjoyed by many."

The food in my stomach turned to stone as the reality of his words sank in. He did not say it, but the gravity in his voice indicated that surviving this period had come at a huge physical and possibly spiritual cost.

Mom pulled three sticks of incense made from recycled prayer flowers out of her bag and gave them to Pak Surya. "This may not ease the pain for you, but sometimes it helps make it more bearable. If you want, we could light these and make an offering," she said.

Pak Surya and Jendra accepted her incense, their faces tight masks of closed emotion. They produced some squares of woven pandan leaves filled with prayer flowers and together we lit the incense and quietly honored the dead.

When the incense had burned, Pak Surya turned to us and said, "Now, I believe you've come here to ask us some questions?"

Mom straightened and got right to it. "We've been hired by Sea Debris to locate an engineer who goes by the name Pertiwi." Mom took out her tablet and shared the photo and information on physical appearance that Betty and Arnold had provided. "Do you know anyone who fits this description?" Mom asked.

Pak Jendra excused himself and took away our dishes. Pak Surya cupped his chin in thought. After a long pause, he said, "These people who hired you—Sea Debris? What do they want with Pertiwi?" He spoke her name with a calmness that revealed little, neither confirming nor denying his knowledge of her.

"They didn't say," Mom replied. "But law enforcement has dramatically changed since the Decree, so I'd venture to guess that at worst they want to press charges and at best they want to pay her off with a nondisclosure agreement."

"You really think they would treat her with the same due process that they show their own citizens?" Pak Surya asked, shaking his head. "Things may have changed since we were young, but people like Pertiwi with fragile immigration statuses are still legally at the mercy of employers and civil servants in their host country."

"That is true," Mom said. "But what we do know is that the technology Pertiwi has had been scheduled to arrive in just a few months in Jakarta. This could mean the difference between just getting by and thriving for lots of people. Not only will more families have access to cheaper and more consistent energy sources, but the inventory for higher-paying jobs will skyrocket while tidal energy units are stationed across the country. You can't deny that this would be great for a lot of people here." She looked around at the people milling outside the pavilion, but I knew she was also thinking of Dad and Arjuna, who taught at the high school but often had to work second jobs to cover energy costs.

Pak Surya gave a heavy sigh. "I cannot answer your original question," he said, "because to do so would break a promise that I made many years ago. But I do not entirely disagree with your logic and will leave you with this: Today, good triumphs over evil. If you follow good, you may find the truth."

When we left the pavilion and were out of earshot of Pak Surya, Mom and I shared our thoughts. "So that was interesting,"

I ventured, feeling somewhat disappointed. "He and Pak Jendra were great company, but that was kind of a bust in terms of leads."

"It did seem that way, didn't it?" Mom said, lost in thought. "But his parting remark has me thinking. It was strange of him to speak in such broad terms of 'good' and 'evil.' I'm still puzzling out what he meant by it."

I rested against the roots of an old banyan tree, feeling tired from the heat and the heavy meal. Scrolling through my phone out of habit, I noticed that the local singer who did acoustic cover songs had made a new post. It was a simple flyer with artistic drawings of traditional Balinese dance superimposed in front of a photo of an old banjar building. Apparently, she was going to be performing tonight in just a few hours.

Mom peered over my shoulder and startled me with a loud gasp. "What?" I asked, mildly annoyed.

She tore the phone from my hands and held it up in the direction of town. "This is the same banjar building as Pak Surya's," she exclaimed. "This singer is going to perform here. Tonight."

We spent the rest of the afternoon doing as much research as we could into the singer before the performance. We learned that her name is Priyanka, she is in her thirties, loves dogs, and grew up in Mimpi. Most of her posts were rather impersonal, but we did come across a photo of her alongside Pak Surya from a few years back. In that post, she gave extensive thanks to Banjar Mimpi for funding her education in Java, which allowed her to receive top-notch professional training from Balinese dance tutors in the capital. There were also a few interview-like posts highlighting some local traditional mask-makers and the lengthy processes that they undertake, including practices for sustainable-wood sourcing, collaboration with priests and community members, and customs to impart respect for spirits throughout the process. There were no other mentions of Pertiwi besides the one, but we suspected nevertheless that Priyanka would be our key to learning more about the missing engineer.

As the sun set, we approached the pavilion-turned-stage and found seating near the back of the growing audience. Gamelan percussion music wafted magnetically from the musicians arranged on the pavilion. Off to the side, a gate façade was propped up, mirroring the entryway common to most temples. The music swelled to a dramatic height and out of the gate the mythical lion Barong emerged, resplendent in gilded clothing and flower-strewn hair. His teeth were larger and wider than the statue version Mom had in our living room, with bulging bright eyes and enormous ears. He pranced playfully with two monkeys, the smoothness of their motions making it easy to forget that it was humans performing this epic dance. Then Rangda, the queen of demons, entered the stage and ensorcelled human soldiers into turning their daggers against their own skin. But as they pierced themselves, Barong cloaked them in protective magic, making them impervious to their deadly weapons. The dance came quickly to an end, with Barong triumphing over Rangda to the cheers of the audience.

"Well, that was fun," I said, tired from a day of dead ends.

"Indeed," Mom said distractedly. She was craning her neck around the crowd of people milling about and talking after the performance. They were distracted and slow-moving in the darkness, possibly out of tiredness but also perhaps due to overindulgence in homemade rice wine as well. Her eyes lit on some movement near the stage, and she zipped in that direction, maneuvering past stumbling shadows with expertise.

"Where are we going?" I called after her.

"Do you know what that dance is about?" she asked me in excitement. "The triumph of good over evil! Pak Surya said that if we found that tonight—"

"Then we should follow the performers who played Barong!" I said, catching on.

We reached the pavilion and rounded toward the back, arriving upon a small gathering of performers and musicians. Some were changing out of their costumes and into more comfortable clothes, while others were enjoying a hot meal and some tea by the fire. Mom's eyes locked on someone removing the Barong mask off in the distance. They were partially shrouded in darkness, but I could see just enough to recognize that it was Priyanka.

She shucked her clothes and folded them carefully into a neat pile, handing them off to someone for storage. We trailed behind at a distance, trying to be as quiet as possible while stumbling through the darkness on unfamiliar terrain. There was not much we could see, but it was obvious from the slope of the ground and the thickness of the air that we were getting closer and closer to sea level. The ground turned from smooth pavement to bumpy packed dirt to shifting sand so suddenly that I had to grab Mom's wheelchair to stop her from pitching over into the darkness.

Then a bright light flashed in our eyes and a jagged edge pressed into my chest. "Who are you and why are you following me?" a harsh voice demanded. Blinking rapidly to get my vision back, I realized that the voice belonged to Priyanka. It was jarring to go from admiring someone's singing voice to fearing them over the course of twenty-four hours, but Mom kept her cool and replied to her.

"We mean you no harm," Mom said. "We're just detectives, looking to track down some proprietary information. All we want is to have a conversation and find out what you know."

"Proprietary information," someone said in the darkness. They did not approach us, but I had a good idea who we were finally speaking with.

"That would indicate ownership of something," they continued. "But how does ownership manifest? If a company funds research, but the scientist creates, tests, and finalizes the technology, does it belong to the company that paid for it or the scientist who made it? What about the community that raised and invested in that scientist? If a coastal town is forced to build a tidal-energy station without being asked or consulted with, and that equipment damages that town and its ecosystem, then who takes ownership and responsibility for correcting those damages?"

"Those are all very thoughtful questions," Mom said slowly. "But it doesn't provide an alternative. Yes, there are flaws with the way big companies like Sea Debris operate. But they have a measurable positive impact on the environment, increasing access to better-paying jobs, and pushing Decree-like world-changing solutions."

"But those solutions don't impact everyone the same," Priyanka said. "Sea Debris designed and tested the tidal-energy stations to be perfect in the Netherlands. But that one-size-fits-all approach is doomed to fail without the proper adjustments."

"They wanted to implement these stations across several islands in Indonesia," the shadowy figure said. "Without consulting with any of those communities. But over the course of a few weeks, we've been able to connect with people from different islands and tweak the tidal-energy stations to suit their unique wave power, depth, wildlife, and fishing needs. All it took was having conversations and inviting people to lean on their expertise to come up with their own solutions."

Mom and I exchanged a look and the shadowy figure receded further into the darkness. Priyanka looked at us and asked, "So now what will you do?"

A few weeks later, Mom and I were sitting in the living room of our boat home having tea with Betty and Arnold.

"You're telling me she fell off a cliff?" Betty said with no small amount of horror.

Mom looked solemnly into her teacup and shuddered. "It was

horrific to watch. She'd been so close to the edge when we caught up to her, but the soil must have been loose because it crumbled right before our eyes."

"We reached for her, but by then it was too late," I said.

Betty and Arnold looked at each other with barely hidden discontent. They opened Pertiwi's case file, which had been updated by us that morning, and moved it from "active" to "archived." "Is there anything else you learned in your investigation?" Arnold asked, voice brightening with a last-ditch dash of hope.

Mom looked at the Barong statue, which had been recently repaired with painstaking care and restored to its former glory. It was now fastened securely within one of the clear, enclosed cabinets where it would be safe from any future falls.

"No," Mom said. "Nothing at all."

EL, THE PLASTOTROPHS, AND ME

Tehnuka

THE WEEK WE WERE APPROVED, YOSHI AND AROHA SHOOK THE dust out of Tara's old baby clothes and El travelled ten days to Whangārei to talk to the medics.

We could have telecommed, but we don't have specialist medics in Kirikiriroa and she wanted training at the hospital. Travel was an attraction, too. In our community, she's the one who most likes time alone in the forest or the trailside gardens.

In typical energetic El mode, she gathered a good stock of herbs on the journey, spent days reading books and talking to their specialists, wove a wahakura for the baby in the evenings with the help of her host whānau, and brought everything back along with new stories of her trip. The flax bassinet was full of extra soap, meds, and cleaning alcohol from the Whangārei co-op. As a supercommunity, they manufactured medication right there. El told several stories and traded Aroha's fabric weaving, and they willingly offered the rest for the new baby.

Unloading the waka, I almost hit myself in the face with the med containers. When I pick them up, they are so lightweight.

"El, is this . . . plastic?"

She grins, turning one over in her hand. "So eco, eh? We'll have to take them up north when we're done, but it's easier than glass to carry. The old State Highway 1 isn't in a great state to push a cart. It would have taken forever."

New plastic is rare. Normally we find it in scraped, dirty pieces when we're working the garden, or washed into the gully after a big storm. The Pukete boy she travelled with laughs when I press on the sides of a transparent bottle, watching it deform inward.

The kaumātua mulled over our application for two years, first observing us with little Tara. Watching us go about daily tasks, how we interacted with the community. They met in the library with kaumātua from small co-ops nearby, and telecommed with the supercommunities on the radio. We knew what to expect from Tara's conception approval, but Yoshi became anxious as months passed.

"What if they approve it and then, you know."

"What, turns out after all those times you suddenly stop enjoying sex?" We don't completely ration contraceptives—better to generate unnecessary waste than unnecessary people. The former, we have ethical, albeit energy-intensive, ways to manage. But I prefer to limit resource consumption. It was no secret he minded the waiting more than I did.

"No, what if we don't conceive? What if we're bad parents?"

"What if they turn us down?" I answered, and he shrugged.

The sunny week before our final hui, the elders had telecomms every day, even international calls requesting up-to-date census stats. El said they stopped when it got cloudy only to conserve batteries. So much thought over a baby, but our kaumātua are more cautious about modelling responsible citizenship since we donated the plastotrophs.

It was the plastotrophs that saved the world from us humans— them, alongside their carbon-fixing counterparts. Amma always said our motivation to change the way we lived was stimulated by seeing the tiniest of life-forms fight to undo our damage. That it gave us the hope we needed to work harder.

But, thanks to another mistake—isn't human history riddled with those?—we'd donated the Kirikiriroa digester to the cleanup of Tāmaki Makaurau.

Tāne, one of our kaumātua, had suggested early on that they should let the microbial population shrink slowly as the initial remediation mahi eased off. But the rehabbers had been strong and eager, and a visiting group finished digging out the main city dump. Good for local decon, but suddenly there was little left to feed the thriving bacterial colony. When site remediation was nearly done the workers moved on and we were short of people to find and rehab the smaller dumps. The three Kirikiriroa communities that shared the digester were all in the same waka: not enough humans to keep up with the microbes. When they realized, it was too late.

So, years before I was born, they'd dismantled everything, paddled and carried it to Tāmaki Makaurau, where the metropolitan cleanup operators gladly took the microbes.

"We learned once again," Amma would say, "the risks of overconsumption. Don't you forget, e hine."

Not forgetting is ultimately part of the kaumātua's role. They provide oversight, remembering what happened generations ago, reading books in te whare pukapuka. That is one building we do maintain. Local communities care for it, while other ramshackle blocks are left in anticipation of a time when they can be safely dismantled and recycled.

When the three of us finally sat on the first floor of the house of books, facing the elders, my stomach flip-flopped through the opening karakia. After a quiet "āmene" I studied the tiled floor, the back of Aroha's shirt, the humming mosquito on my knee—anything to avoid looking at Koro Tāne during his kōrero about guarding the land and what it offered wisely, about being able to support the workers who would one day come to dismantle the concrete city and its rotting suburbs.

I recalled Amma's story of King Dasaratha. He had to do a

whole yāgam, summoning the spirit of fire to get his three wives pregnant with four sons. That was only the start of the whole saga, because Kaikeyi became jealous and wanted her son on the throne instead of Rama. At least we only had to meet with the elders.

They talked about Amma's contribution to the co-op. How a lizard conservator from Te Waipounamu had been willing to uproot herself and her infant daughter to meet their needs. Amma spent her childhood with little blue penguins, her early career with cold-blooded reptiles, then moved across the strait to try being an ecologist.

I'm hardly a credit to generations of scientists. One tipuna worked on the possum sterilization campaign down south. A great-grandparent led the native parrot rescue. That's about all I know of my whakapapa. And here I was, reluctantly planting vegetable gardens and harvesting orchards in a land to which I had no whānau or ancestral ties.

The kaumātua addressed each of us and our backgrounds, but Aroha and Yoshi were proud to hear theirs. They belonged to the local hapū. They belonged here.

I ended up staring at my torn nails, trying to love a future spent looking after someone else's child, picking at a callous in the crease of my thumb and . . .

"Malar!" Yoshi grabbed my hand, his crooked-toothed smile the most beautiful thing I'd ever seen.

"We look forward to welcoming our newest mokopuna," Tāne

finished. I was too stunned to talk. Aroha responded with an eloquent acknowledgement of their concerns and our gratitude for a chance to contribute to the future of our people.

The kaumātua gave us their blessing and suggested waiting a few weeks so the baby was less likely to be born in midwinter. Aroha's kuia remembers feeding the last synthetic sleeping bags and jackets to the composter when they fell apart too much to salvage, and though summers are warm we do see winter frosts. They say it's a harder life in our small co-ops, but we have the satisfaction of contributing that experience to the supercommunities as they make their slower transitions toward living lightly. That's what brought Amma here.

El stood in the shade chatting to a young guy who'd just joined the Pukete co-op up the river. She asked, "Well? Will I visit the medics up north?" and hugged the three of us in turn.

The Pukete boy had business upriver too. Once he'd offered congratulations, he suggested they travel together. "Cen't be arsed the planting," he said.

El said he was lovely. She'd spent the hour outside learning to understand his accent, so we took her word for it. He did skive off planting the next day to go trading, likely landing himself in trouble with his own co-op, then waited for El camped by te awa near Mercer while she continued her journey on foot.

I envied her the peace of the forest, although I knew after the winter rains she'd be trudging through swamp, tall flax and fluffy toetoe and mud, from when she left the canoe until she got up onto the hills. They rowed back to our landing at the Old Gardens a few weeks later.

As we unpack, with them laughing at my reaction to plastic bottles, El tells us about the megacity dotted with small volcanoes that haven't erupted for hundreds of years, how you can walk up onto the highest, still clear of the regenerating forest, and look all around at the remnant metropolis. How they have giant windgens, and sail around the harbour as they've been doing for two and a half centuries. Most are temporary workers with family in Whangārei or Te Paeroa-a-Toi. "We could go too, Malar," she says. "Some stay years, but some only stay three months."

Yoshi and I haven't travelled. He says it's ancestral memory; our families came escaping what their homes had become, while El's came because they were navigators and explorers, or thought life would be better in the colonial frontiers, and that's why she's always in search of something new. I never tell Yoshi he's talking nonsense. Some of his tīpuna came to escape rising seas, and it makes sense to him that's why he belongs inland. My ancestors, those I know of, were in Aotearoa twice as many generations back, but I'm still a foreigner, especially without Amma. I have to justify my presence, my appearance, the traditions no one here recognizes.

Yoshi likes to stay home, digging in the garden, and I stay too. This morning, mid-January, I'm turning over the compost.

The others go off whenever they want. Upriver, up the mountain; whatever they want to do, they ask permission when they need with the confidence they'll get it. Today, though, we all have mahi here.

A few earthworms drop onto the grassy patch beside the heap and I gather them one by one, poking a stick under each wriggling body, thinking my clumsy fingers will squash them. Yoshi laughs at my caution.

He and Aroha had to talk me into applying to the co-op, even though I was the one who was supposed to have the baby. As the last worm slinks into the soil, I wonder if having a baby raised by people who belong here will make me feel like I belong. I wonder if that's why they suggested I should do it, or if that's why I agreed to—because a pregnancy on behalf of the co-op would make me feel like I'd earned my right to live here. I put the shovel back in the lean-to and go to build the fire.

Pongal was a harvest festival for Amma, even though it's summer in Aotearoa. It was the only thing she celebrated, other than a two-hundred-year-old Martyrs' Day for a war her tīpuna had fled, and Matariki that we all observe when Matariki, the Pleiades constellation, or karthikei, as Amma called it, first appears in the midwinter sky.

In the old days they boiled rice, milk, and jaggery—fresh produce of the land. This country was once known for its cows' milk, though the other ingredients would have been imported. Now, we grow rice in the wet peatland soils that used to be a reservoir for effluent. They still keep captive cows overseas, in small numbers. We chose not to keep them at all. Amma was vegan, so I never sweeten the rice with honey but, as I do every year, I watch the pot of plain rice froth over and say "pongal o pongal." This time, I wonder if our baby will one day do the same.

Someone, somewhere on the other side of the world, must celebrate a traditional Pongal, know how to say, "When Thai is born, a way is born" in Tamil, have people around them who'll understand. They must remember the stories Amma told me. Properly, not vague fragments of the Ramayanam, or why Pillayar had an elephant face, which I've forgotten. At least no one will know or care if I do a half-arsed job of the celebration. Traditions change, right?

El joins in, saying "pongal o pongal" with us, and takes a handful of rice before going for a swim, while we spend the afternoon cleaning and rearranging the rooms. Aroha shakes out the mats, I sweep, and Yoshi goes down to the river to wash the linen. We are fortunate to have the three of us, and all the extended whānau. Amma hadn't found it easy trying to care for me and go about her work. I remember Aroha's kuia putting me to bed and feeding me my morning porridge almost as clearly as I remember Amma doing the same.

My pulse has been fluttering in my stomach for weeks, since the hui, like it has only done once before when I fell in love with Yoshi. This summer day, putting our whare in order, is the most I've ever felt at home. We hang the washing together, and Aroha buries some potatoes to cook while we lie in the evening sun waving away midges and singing.

Yoshi sleeps late the next morning. We leave him, take apples and machetes, and go with others from our co-op to clear a trail south of the river and scope out the old railway line. One day, when the rare earths problem is solved, we are supposed to have public transport across the country. None of us believe it, not when we see the rusty iron tracks and collapsing embankments, but our job is to monitor and advise, not make decisions for someone a hundred years from now.

We return sweaty and scratched from tugging at gorse—one of those invasive species we haven't yet got under control—and jump in the river. The water is cool. I could float here forever listening to the tūī warbling, until Aroha starts complaining about bugs. The two of us say ka kite and walk back over the hill, the earth sun-warmed under our feet, and at home we find Yoshi huddled on his mat with a fever.

Infections aren't uncommon, but Aroha catches them so easily that I send her to stay in the marae in case it's contagious. I spend the evening brewing mānuka infusions for Yoshi and contemplating the cooking fire. Moving away from fossil fuels sent us back to burning dry wood, but El says in some supercommunities they still have induction hobs. In the long wait for the pot to boil, I try to imagine one. It seems as magical as an island fished from the sea, or a talking monkey that flies, or hundreds of people in one place, travelling in metal airplanes that crisscross the sky leaving long trails of condensation. I've seen a photo of that in the archive room, and of a graveyard of grounded aircraft somewhere up north. I guess no one cared to preserve a picture of a piece of metal that invisibly heated water.

In the morning Aroha leaves two bowls of kai and a deck of cards on the porch, but I can't remember the rules for playing solitaire. By lunchtime I convince Yoshi to sit outside with me and drink his lukewarm soup. "I've got the worst headache," he says. Two mouthfuls in, he clutches his stomach and returns to his mat. To distract myself I build a house of cards in the front room and go to pick tomatoes. It's so warm they've begun rotting on the vine. Tedious weather for Yoshi to be wrapped up in blankets, but it's no better when his chills give way to a sweat. He asks for cold water, "instead of that *aluppu* leaf tea." One more reason to love him: he comes out with forgotten Tamil like that, words he picked up from me and Amma years ago, though I've not spoken it with anyone since she died.

River water's good, but the rainwater tank is safer since his stomach's unhappy. But when I go to fill the earthenware jug, it's swarming with a quiet hum from big mozzies, not just sandflies. I leave the boiled infusion to cool in the shade instead. He doesn't complain at the taste or the warmth, and that bothers me. I sit next to him with a wet cloth, humming waiata to which I've forgotten the words in three languages.

El and her mother visit in the evening with a glass thermometer and med supplies. The draught blows my card construction over when they walk in. Yoshi grumbles at being woken, and when they leave again in twenty minutes to radio up north.

A ruru's hoot rouses me from the porch. I'm too tired to do more than check on Yoshi inside and chew on a twig to clean my teeth before sleeping. They don't return until morning, when they wake him calling from the porch. I'm out back cooking the watery rice kanjee Amma used to make when I was sick.

"The good news is," El's mother begins cheerily, "they had ideas of what it might be. But you'll need a blood test."

Neither of us has taken a blood test before. They're used in supercommunities where labs are available. Isolated co-ops may have shared facilities for emergencies. But who ever heard of taking a blood test for influenza, or a cold?

El and her mum, apparently. Though Yoshi has enough appetite for his kanjee this morning, they insist he should be tested.

"He's improving. If he has to travel, he won't be able to rest." The nearest place with a laboratory would be one of the cleanup camps at Tāmaki Makaurau.

"He'll get better medical care there, Malar." El's mum rubs my back and I flinch away.

"What if it's contagious? Will we all have to go up north for tests?"

Yoshi adds, "I'd rather wait it out here," and gives me his bowl before returning to his mat. "I want to sleep. Not paddle up the river, and walk what, two days?"

El and her mum exchange a look. Auntie says, "The difficulty is that it might not be something that you can wait out so easily. Wait until you feel a little better, yes. It's fortunate your symptoms are mild."

"This is mild?"

"You've noticed the bugs this year, no? There are mosquito-borne parasites and viruses they have on record, and . . ."

That makes no sense. "Malaria was eradicated centuries ago," I protest. "Like smallpox and polio and . . ."

El corrects me that malaria only disappeared 150 years ago, and there are, she says, a googol type of infections and ways they could spread. A couple of cases have been reported up north, so we don't have much choice. The medics have to see for themselves. Her mother adds that it might be a good chance to get some tests myself since we haven't conceived yet, have we? She's probably snooped around back and seen my menstrual cloths drying outside.

"Mum!"

"Oh, look, El, she may as well have the tests. We can't be purists about downscaling tech. We're not pioneers or colonists. We can actually ask for help."

I stand, taking the bowl to wash. "They told us it could take months to get pregnant anyway. I'll talk to Yoshi about all that later."

El leaves some ginger that she says is good to make tea for nausea. "Sorry about Mum. Let me know whenever you're ready to go."

*   *   *

It's a week before Yoshi agrees to travel. His fever has been coming and going, but he has more energy now. El and the Pukete boy take the oars to start, and we swap during the day. Waikato Te Awa flows fast, offering a calm I never find elsewhere. A flock of rosellas—those colorful squawky parrots brought from across the ocean in the twentieth century, sometime between the invasion of the English and the welcome swallows—flies past. Yoshi, who rarely comes on the river, finds the energy to point out kōtare, long beaks and turquoise-blue feathers with a flash of orange, on overhanging branches. Eels in the water. Koi, too, gleaming gold but another introduced species. Aroha always says she hates these exotic pests, but what does a fish know of four hundred years of colonization? For that matter, what do we?

We stay overnight in a hut El knows from previous trips. The boy jumps off onto a narrow trail, to let the neighbors know we're passing through. It's a half-hour walk and they won't notice we're here, but it is tika to inform them.

While Yoshi goes to rest, we pull the boat onto shore and unload. I begin searching the bush for dry wood, gathering it into the base of my shirt.

"Malar, I have to tell you something." El isn't smiling.

I drop the kindling. "Is it about the infection? Is it serious?" I hadn't been too worried, even after they said that about mosquitoes. Stressed about the trip, about making Yoshi travel, sure, but he seems happy. They didn't make it sound dangerous, only like something that needed study . . .

"No."

"About the two of you, then?" I should have known it would be about that boy.

She sits on a knobby tree root and rubs her hand over it. "No. Sort of."

It might be the way she talked about the ginger tea, or how she exclaimed, "Mum!" when the topic of conception came up, but I'm not that surprised when she says, "He doesn't know yet, no one does, but . . ."

For the tiniest moment I want to stop her, as if not hearing it would make it okay. I don't want to deal with a disaster someone else has created.

Aren't we all dealing with the disasters someone else has created?

She finishes, "I think I'm pregnant," and though I'm expecting it I stare as if I'm not. What does she want from me? Reassurance?

"A couple of months. I'm sorry," she adds. From her trip to Whangārei.

The kindest response would be that she doesn't have to apologize. In another country, even in some of our Aotearoa supercommunities, it might not matter. They have leeway—unexpected births and deaths, arrivals and departures, and don't wait for one to allow the other, only track that it balances out. Those in our co-ops are invited through their parents' application for a birth or through a request for a worker, like Amma had. Couldn't she have waited until they were back home with contraception? Or had theirs failed? We're told it can happen.

Does it make any difference why? We knew it might take months to conceive, that it might not happen at all. But that was a possibility, not a certainty. What's certain is that El's having the next baby in the co-op.

I take a few steps away. There's nowhere else to sit among flax and brush. I don't want to ask these questions. I want her to have told someone else first, to not know about it until I stop getting my periods too, and no one could expect us to give up our chance.

Amma taught me to think carefully. Sometimes it means I think too much. Sometimes it means I know how to respond. "Give me some time, yeah? Don't tell Yoshi until he's better."

My hands shake when I start gathering twigs again. El continues silently, staying well away. Another thing I don't want: to keep secrets. The worry starts piling up so that my hands sweat against the bark and my linen shirt is too stuffy. If this is going wrong, what else? What about Yoshi's illness? What will Aroha say? We've always been close. Even more so in the last years, planning to co-parent. She doesn't want a partner, but she does want a baby in her family. I dump my kindling beside the firepit, letting twigs bounce and scatter, and go to wash in the river.

Yoshi doesn't notice anything wrong during the meal, so I know he's exhausted. I've hardly talked to the Pukete boy. I'd had a vague idea that I should earlier, because El cared about him. Now,

I don't want to see his face. It's not his fault any more than El's, but when the rain starts to pour that night and I'm stuck in the hut crying into my arms I wish he'd stayed where he came from, not answered whatever need Pukete had for a guy who wanted to skive off planting, spend all his time on the river, and donate sperm where it wasn't needed.

Yoshi's snuffling in his sleep, and what is normally endearing makes me want to hit something. This little hut can only support so much of my tension. I go outside, sheltering among trees whose names Amma would have known, and water drips down them so I'm wet anyway. Amma would tell me to go back inside and dry off before I get sick. That's what I want to tell my pillai one day: stories of many-headed gods and nonsense about the cold making you sick. I want Aroha to tell her kuia's myths about the taniwha in te awa, and Yoshi to teach the language of plants. But our hypothetical child might never exist, and that's what I think about in the rain.

Kaikeyi demands, in the Ramayanam, that her son become the next king. That his half brother Rama, the rightful crown prince, be exiled to the forest. Kausalya, Rama's mother, has to let him go. Who do I become if I demand to keep our right to raise a nonexistent child over El's, sanctioned or not? Who do I become if I don't?

There's limited space. For my anger in that hut. For children in our co-op. For bacteria in the digester. El will have her baby. The rest of us might be packed off like the plastotrophs to Tāmaki Makaurau, where they can afford to support another child. I begin shivering.

There was a slogan in the old days: "There is no Planet B." As kaitiaki we still make mistakes. Inside our co-ops, we forget the world outside isn't an endless resource.

In te marama's rising light, rain turns to mist and a cricket croaks in branches overhead. Our experiment is failing. We co-ops are reliant on the resources of supercommunities. We, who are supposed to lead the way, cling to them, treating them as our Planet B. Medical help, lab tests, overflow when we can't feed our digester, factories to make what we aren't ready to cope without. Amma left them, thinking the future was devolution. But if we in the co-ops refuse to live independently, kaitiakitanga will be left to the supercommunities. We're failing as guardians. Failing, and modelling failure.

No one comes to find me. Shivering, I return and dry off. The moonlight is bright through my eyelids, but I can't sleep anyway.

The next day everyone pretends not to notice my tears when I'm paddling. Or maybe they really don't notice. But when we stop for a break on the riverside Yoshi asks quietly if I'm ill. "I'm feeling better, if you're worried." He squeezes my hand. "You're worried about something."

I hate not telling him, more than I hate what's happened. As I break up the rēwena bread, I talk instead about last night's thoughts. That we've wasted the effort of generations denying themselves luxuries of technology, children, whatever else they

have in supercommunities to live in the middle of nowhere thinking we were leading the way forward.

"Why wasted? Because we're going to their medics for help?"

"That, and needing people like Amma coming from supercommunities to help us, and because we couldn't even keep our
digester."

He picks up his chunk of parāoa rēwena. "You're worrying about
what's next. That's not wrong, but it's a balance, Malar. Everyone
living as we do won't work perfectly. Look at anyone who needs
meds or tech to get by. We're finding out what's truly essential,
yes. It's taken this long already, though." He takes a mouthful
and I watch him chew, wondering how I'll tell him. "You know
it won't happen overnight. We need to worry about the world as
it is now, not only what it becomes in a year or a hundred. You
think whatever it was that crawled out of the primordial ooze and
evolved us gave a shit about what you'd become?" Another mouthful. I'm glad he has his appetite back.

"Even the digester," he says. "We could watch it die as a matter of principle, or we could realize we screwed up and give it to
someone who could use it. Treating our rohe as too much of a
closed system is as dangerous as considering the world an endless
resource."

He understands me, one of the infinite reasons I love him. And
he's right. I don't kiss him, because he's chewing, but shift closer
and watch the ducks ignoring us on the other side of the river.

The plastotrophs showed up when we needed them, an

ecosystem responding to the world around it. The carbon fixers might have been there all along. Now they are symbiotic communities working together in equilibrium, to solve our problems. Els and Yoshis and Pukete boys, even Malarkal who think they don't belong. Supercommunities and co-ops.

There will be places we're useful. Back in Kirikiriroa. Or anywhere. Each place holds a different future. I'm not tangata whenua and don't have land to belong to, but I belong with Yoshi and Aroha, in any land with people who'll have me.

I lead us back to the water. There's grey light through clouds, the current of the river, and new places to see.

CANVAS—WAX—MOON

Ailbhe Pascal

CANVAS

It's early in the morning, but Neya and I are already racing to be the first one to lace up boots and tool pouches and then step out into the Alley. His leather boots are identical in make and wear to mine, but my canvas pouch is a deep blue to his sun-bleached bag, and my harvest scissors are always kept sharp. If I had my brother's forearms, maybe I wouldn't mind letting my tools go dull every now and then either. Builders can be such showoffs.

"Hey, do you have the list?" Neya asks, barely audible.

I do a double take, then shake my head. "Nice try getting me to slow down," I say, punctuating it with the knot at the top of my left boot, confident this was my race to win.

"No, I'm being serious," he laughs and holds up his hands. "Time out?"

"Okay, okay." I also lift my hands from boot-tying and meet his concerned gaze. "I watched you borrow a quill from Grams yesterday, so I assumed you wrote it all down."

"I know I'm the oldest, but why do you always assume I've got your notes?" I want to say it's because I don't feel well, because I'm a Pisces moon, because he *likes* taking notes—and because this time I asked him to—but I just raise my eyebrow at him. "Well?" I ask after a moment. "And you're just barely older, don't give me that."

"Three years isn't 'barely older.' But, yeah," he grins. "I've got . . . it . . . right . . . here." Neya draws out his words as he takes a paper from behind him and dangles it in my face. It's our list in his distinct scrawl.

"Why'd you ask, then?" I suck my teeth.

"Cuz I made you stop . . ." With that he eyes his feet. His crow friend, Unbelievable, finished his lacing for him. I punch his arm again, this time harder. "Ow," he laughs, Unbie cackling with him. "Hit me any harder and we'll wake up Grams and Jidda." His indignant smirk gets a rise out of me and he knows it.

"Ugh!" I shout in my loudest whisper. "I can't *believe* you're pulling this today—of all days!" I still can't help thinking that having a sibling keeps me on my toes.

"Ashix." Pa Opelie steps lovingly into the lamplight, his voice a drum. Neya and I immediately stop fussing. "There is nothing to be nervous about," he continues. "Not today. I think ole Unbelievable here is merely reminding you to let others *help* you, baby." I roll my eyes, but love my cheeseball pa all the same. "And look!" He lifts his face to the windows behind us. "It's a *beautiful* sunrise." Faint light has just barely started filling the sky, and I let myself believe a good day is coming. After a moment, the shimmering bird gives a long caw. "You're right," Pa chuckles with the crow in understanding. "Singing is also good for a morning like this."

I stand from my lacing chair. "Yeah, but you're a *morning* person, Pa, and you're not feeling nauseous to your toes."

He chuckles and turns to Neya. "Will you help your sibling find good things to remember about today?" He's speaking in a stage whisper, still smiling.

"Hey, I'm right here!" I say, shaking my head with a laugh. I feel lucky that my family is working so hard to make today easy for me, and I'm honestly looking forward to this little adventure, but come *on*, I'm less than a foot away from either of them.

"I'll sing all their favorite songs," Neya promises, as if I hadn't interrupted. Pa nods wordlessly and gives him a gentle pat on the back.

The two have the same warm olive complexion, but look different in most every other way: Neya's tall and wiry, Pa is short and stout; Neya *always* looks like he just rolled out of bed, Pa always looks like he's coming out of meditation; and Neya's eyes are gray-green like mine and our Nopa's, Pa's eyes are a bright hazel. I, on the other hand, have Pa's build, Nopa's wheat tone, and, mysteriously, the same raised, stone-shaped birthmark on my mid-back that Nopa does. I just spent the sleepless night wondering how exactly a birthmark gets passed down like that.

Yet I have a cane that's all my own. I considered taking it today, but I have a feeling my legs will manage on adrenaline alone. I lace my arms through my canvas pouch's two arm straps, tying them across my heart, and let out a sigh.

Pa steps from Neya to me. "I love you, my witching-hour baby," he says. I look into his opening arms and accept his hug. I murmur into his warm, cedar-scented sweater: "I love you too, Opelie." Neya wraps both of us in his arms and gives a squeeze.

When we let go, I bend down to kiss the top of Unbelievable's head and we head off into the Alley.

I've been enjoying the birds-at-dawn chorus, letting the music fill me, but not yet ready to sing like Pa suggested I should. Even with the sunrise barely peeking out, even after only fifteen-some-odd minutes in the Alley, I already see someone we know coming toward us down the corridor. She's walking easy and waving hello. Immediately, I cover my face and duck behind Neya, but I know it's too late. "Mornin', Laurel!" Neya shouts. "Haven't seen you in a while."

Now we're face-to-face, so I straighten up, pretending like I wasn't just hiding from her. I'm not smooth, but I'm too flustered to care.

"Yeah, *shit*," she replies in a low voice. "How you been, Neya?"

Her mellow voice settles in me warm and sweet. I blush. I was afraid of this interaction, afraid it would make me second-guess everything, but I want to be part of this conversation too. *You got this*, I silently tell myself.

The corvids of the Alley are gathering on a nearby cable line, sharing gossip-glances with Unbie and unabashedly listening to Laurel. She easily keeps pace with Neya's chit-chatting, but her eyes stay on me, and I blush deeper red. "Hey, Laurel . . ." I finally pipe up. "What are you . . . What brings you to the Alley so early?" I gesture awkwardly with my arm, like she's never seen the Alley before. Amusement dances at the corners of her lips, and I duck my head into the turtle shell of my shoulders. Neya gives me a curious glance like, *Why are you talking like this, nerd?*

"The Alley is the shortcut to the River from my house," she answers calmly. I'm zeroed in on her presence. "I meet the fishermen down there on Tuesdays to talk Maroon business."

The Maroon Society has independent affairs, networks, traditions, and happenings. Non-Black folk like Neya and I know that much, and we also know to respect Maroon privacy. I kick up some mulch knowing I have no right asking her to go another way and still wishing we hadn't run into each other in the thick of my current . . . tasks.

I *so* want to tell her everything. I want to hear Laurel's laugh again. But I'm not ready to see her yet, and everything that could've been is hitting me all at once. "Well, I hope you enjoy the sunshine by the water," Neya is saying. "It's going to be a beautiful one."

"Thank you, Neya," Laurel says, moving easefully past us. My eyes begin to sting as I turn to watch as she continues on her way. I want to run up and ask to hold her hand. I want to go back to springtime. Before we knew I'd leave.

And before I had to come back.

Neya nudges me and we walk the other way for a few minutes, his arm still around my shoulders. Neither the crunching leaves underfoot nor the morning cacophony above us is loud enough to drown out my racing heart.

He finally asks, "What was up with you back there? You were almost scared to be seen."

"Akhi, I really don't wanna talk about it right now."

"Laurel is the girl from across the Creek who came to all the summer mud parties by the River, right? Double Sag?"

"Neya," I warn. "Change the subject."

Silence lingers for a second before Neya elbows me hard. "She only talked to me cuz I was walking with you, Ash. You should go visit her sometime."

"I don't even know . . ." I pull my cowl over my nose.

"I do," he interrupts, using his I'm-being-helpful voice. "She's up on the East-West road that runs past the swimming hole. You'll know her house by its lavender door."

I try not to show that I *know* where she lives. It's *how to go back* that I haven't figured out yet.

I need something to distract me—and to keep Neya from asking anything else. "Okay, okay, let me see that list again," I say.

He shrugs, then slides out of his left pouch strap, slinging the canvas to his front to reach in for the prized paper. As he hands it over, he says, "I think our first stop is the House of Grandmothers."

WAX

Old Mellie is also lovingly called the Mint Queen. When people were still proposing ideas for the first wave of repurposing old state buildings, Mellie was there with her pun cap on: "What if we turned the old moneyhouse into a *green*house?" she'd asked the gathered neighbors. The stories say that some people laughed in delight, and some people laughed because they saw a young Boricua with a cane steadying her stance. People didn't see the magic in so many of us back then. Some people still don't.

But our family does. "Mellie's eyes were full with a clear, serious vision," Grandma Sylvia has described. "There would be dozens of these gatherings around the city, where everyone's ideas were given room to breathe. Hers is one of the many visions we celebrate today."

"Bless the vision of our elders," Neya and I recited decorously.

"You know, starting something you've always wanted to do is exhilarating," Grams continued. "But starting something new can feel frightening." Mellie must have been so brave to propose an idea in front of everyone like that. "Some people would say something so experimental it would feel *impossible*."

The last word was an invitation for Neya and me to speak with her, to imagine what *impossible* felt like back then. We've heard her story before, but speaking important words together helps us become the spell.

"Hearing so many *new* ideas out loud would give me goosebumps," Jidda Warda added. "Mellie's proposal was like that: it was life, children. In the parks and halls we gathered in, people usually couldn't sit still, and they *wanted, wanted, wanted*. But when Mellie spoke, we gulped like a thirst had been quenched." She inhaled deeply like she was drinking in the air. "My whole spirit said *yes* to her idea, and it made me giddy."

The two of them get wistful telling us this story, no matter how many times they share it with us, because their generation was the first to really change course. They changed how we build, how we treat life, and how we treat ourselves. Witnessing them is the gift of our generation.

Old Mellie has since handed off her passion project to younger folk downtown. A building that used to press metal into coins for a whole country donated its tools to our builders' guilds. The builders then installed glass walls, and only the sprawling mint family were planted inside: apple mint, peppermint, basil, skullcap, thyme, bee balm, sage, oregano, hyssop, horehound . . . Too many to name.

During the warm seasons, the doors are open on all sides of the Mint, so you'll find pigeons and sparrows in the vaulted ceilings, groundhogs exploring for the fun of it, flies and bees buzzing around, and always a new variety of mint.

Grandma Sylvia is partial to Mellie's home apiary *because you can always trust a witch who talks to bees.* And when the nut harvest comes in, Jidda Warda always brings Mellie her first tray of baklawa *because desert is medicine too.* I can hear Grams cooing to Jidda after a family trip to the Mint last year: "Mellie really hasn't lost her sparkle in all these years. You and me," she tutted, "we can get cynical. But Ole Melissa, she's only gotten more curious about the world." They leaned into each other as they walked ahead of me.

A few days ago, I was with Neya and Pa in the apothecary, and Pa was dictating our errands in a meandering order when he finally remembered honey. "Oh, oh!" Grandma hollered from the kitchen next to the apothecary. She had been pretending not to eavesdrop, but we all knew she'd pipe up at some point. "Opelie, you know she'll have the best pennyroyal and motherwort."

Pa looked quizzically at us, so Neya leaned in, covering his mouth from Sylvia's view. "They're both types of mint," Neya whispered, giving Pa a concealed you-got-this thumbs up.

They're also exactly the medicine I need.

I set my mouth in a grim line, but Pa mouthed, "Ooooooh," and nodded cheerfully toward Neya's handwritten list. "We've made a note, Mama," he said aloud to Grams.

* * *

The morning is thick with fog, dew frosting the row-home windows that face the Alley and soaking the vines we wade through. I peer through jeweled webs to wave at a couple doing tai chi in their yard and can't help but laugh at the squirrels romping up tree trunks. Unbelievable has flown off after catching up with the other Alley crows. Everything is velveted by the wet air.

We wade through Mellie's chin-high borders of rosemary, leading from the Alley to her kitchen. As the leaves gently scrape past us, we slow down and remember to receive the spell of protection—from beestings and the evil eye.

"Good morning," we say to the buzzing elders around us. Mellie affectionately calls her bees the "Neighborhood Grandmothers."

"Good morning, sweet ones!" Mellie sings grandly from her chair in her open doorway.

I give a small wave. Neya gives a dramatic bow. I roll my eyes and elbow my brother's side.

"You've come to help me find something," Mellie says.

"Yes, please," Neya says.

"Good, good," she replies offhandedly, wheeling back into the warmth of the House of Grandmothers.

In no time flat, Neya is climbing up on top of a worn stool, pantry doors wide open in front of him. He wobbles on his tippy toes to reach the next shelf, and I have my hands out to spot him. We're helping Mellie find . . . *something*.

"I'm sitting out on the bridge to enjoy the height of it all," Mellie says to no one in particular. Her voice is like a throaty cormorant: a little shaky, a little distant. She goes on: "When a very brave cat nuzzles my back, 'Mmmm,' I say, 'what a good cat, what a lovely cat, up on my chair, so high up where no one but Old Mellie likes to go.'"

Neya shuffles glass jars around in the cupboard and pulls out another unlabeled sack, plopping it on the counter in front of Mellie. "That the one?" he asks, only a little winded. We've been trying—well, *he's* trying—to find Old Mellie's "special flour" for about twenty minutes now, and it's work getting a *bruja* what she wants.

Neya shifts his weight back and forth with impatience, but I motion for him to cool it, pointing to the wobbling stool.

"I notice this cat's swollen look, oh, yes I do," she continues, not responding to his question. "I ask to feel kitty's belly-pouch, ooh silky soft. Sure as sure there are firm, little would-be cats in there, all the way up on the wide, long bridge."

My nausea crashes over me.

I aim for a nearby mop bucket and watch breakfast leave my body. My face feels flushed and sore.

Neya surprises me with a glass of water and an encouraging smile. I wish I had stayed in bed. That night . . . I wish I'd thought . . . I don't know what I could have thought. I made my choices based on a *feeling*.

The air in this kitchen is swamp-heavy, but for a moment, I could feel the ocean breeze from that night tickle the back of my neck.

And I puke again. I know this doesn't faze Mellie, but I feel bare on her floor like this.

Mellie's eyes are closed to receive the warmth of first light from her doorway. "Me-yow!" a tabby calls, bounding through the rosemary and jumping into her lap. They nuzzle the arm of the chair and look at me, still bent over the bucket. I gather myself enough to say, "How do you do?" Not at all my normal voice—why do I put on airs around cats?

Neya giggles and simply says, "Hey there" when Mellie's companion jumps down to welcome us into their home.

"Hmmm," Mellie continues, turned again toward her impossibly deep cupboards. "Tabitha, won't you help me? I'm trying to find that dang flour—you know the one that we only take out on special occasions?"

The cat—Tabitha, I assume—rubs against Mellie's ankles, and the crone reaches down a hand to scratch her friend's chin while she uses her other hand to take the sack Neya last put on the counter and draw it into her lap.

"Maybe it wasn't all for nothing," Neya whispers to me.

I reply with a quiet grunt. *Maybe it wasn't all for nothing.* Is that what I'll be saying in a moon's time?

"You know, that's a good point," Mellie says, probably still to Tabitha. "I was just thinking, if only I remembered where I put my old broom."

Tabitha tilts her head out and Mellie nods seriously in reply. "Hmmm. Gracias, Tabby-nabby." The cat slides her body along Mellie's leg, eyes closed and satisfied before Mellie turns from the cabinets toward the door again.

I'm leaning against Neya, regaining some strength. I'm in no hurry to get off the floor, enjoying the cat-witch banter keeping me from my own thoughts. "Meow?" Tabitha asks.

"Sí, mira, I promise you'll get fish tonight. Now, where was I . . ."

From her broom closet, she tosses a large paper bag of twigs over her shoulder, a clear shot through her open Alley-facing door to the top of the compost pile on the side of her ramp. Then she wheels closer to the back of her closet and pulls the light chain to appraise her shelves up close.

"Bruja Melissa," Neya says, in a voice that betrays his impatience, "how can I help?" He stands just to the side of the open door.

"Take this home," she says directly, digging out a small wooden box from the back shelf.

I'm standing with Neya now, peering into the small space. There are a dozen boxes like it, lined neatly, if a little dusty. Mellie gives an *ahem* and we make room for her to back out of the closet.

Once she's out, Mellie hands me the little box with the sack of flour on top. The case is held closed by a blot of beeswax at the top; it smells of honey and is marked with a crescent moon seal. I can only hope it has what Grandma Sylvia meant for us to find with Mellie.

"Ash," Mellie says, putting her hands on mine. "Put your memories in the box when you've emptied it."

I nod my head and accept the spell. "Thank you, bruja Melissa. I will."

MOON

"Kiddo, you warm enough?" Pa's holding a folded blanket.

I've been staring at the moon, running the day's errands through my mind. *Did we get everything? Am I ready?*

Pa's question pulls me back to my body. "Yeah, I'm alright," I say, rubbing my arms across my chest. "It's less than a moon past the equinox anyway."

"Suit yourself," he says, shrugging slightly. He piles the blanket back into his lap and faces the fire again. "Omi, this is a beautiful fire. What a good idea." He smiles and slumps a little in the warmth.

Jidda Warda gives a nod of acknowledgment from the other side of the pit, reserved as always. "Mmh. Fire is good for circulation, and circulation is just what Ash needs right now."

Pa replies by tapping his temple to say *Got it*. I won't be the last one coming to him, the new apothecary apprentice, for help like this.

Looking at our family, a dozen or so of my relatives around the fire, my chest tightens. I wanted to be *grown up* by now, not to need so much support navigating life. I'm eating slower than everyone else. My head hurts, and my stomach definitely hasn't been cooperative lately. My jaw slackens and sobs tumble out of me.

Everyone stops their chattering to witness me, and I wish they wouldn't. I want to be held and I want to be alone at the same time. How is that possible? How is any of this possible?

How had I been so reckless?

Jidda Warda throws eucalyptus in the fire and joins Grandma Sylvia under their blanket. The fragrant smoke means something to them in their secret language, invented during decades of shared ritual. I know that some of their language is my inheritance, a special thing for us family here to witness and make our own meanings from. The incense reminds me of the first spells I was ever taught to cast, and I let myself be enveloped by it.

At first, the blood comes easy, like a regular period. But now it is hot and thick, and tearing out of me like I've never known before. My pants are unbuttoned and stuffed full of rags. My shirt is at the foot of my bed with my favorite wool sweater, tangled up with my bedding. My insides are messy right now; it feels right that my outsides should be too. In a clay dish at the windowsill, mugwort ash is piled high from many nights of burning before bed.

Jidda Warda places a jar on my bedside table, the sturdy glass brimming with well water, and she wordlessly settles beside me. She tucks loose strands of hair behind my ear as I reach for a drink. It's freezing to the touch, so I clench the glass tighter and take the shock head-on.

The well is sweet to drink from, its chill rushing into my chest and falling into my belly. Down, down the water goes, and with it, relief washes over me. From the temples of my forehead, through my unclenching jaw, then down into the spaces between my shoulders, my ribs, my toes . . .

All-encompassing *relief* settles in me as I gather between my legs this confirmation that I am no longer pregnant.

Jidda Warda rubs my back with rosemary oil from Mellie's kit and whispers blessings, her calloused hands slow as she speaks:

"Sweet Ash, you will never have to host Life you do not welcome.

"You will recover to strong and hearty years ahead.

"You have a sacred commitment to listen to your bodymind.

"You inherit the magic of good witches before you.

"You will remember this blood and it will give you your own Life back.

"You are magical . . ."

Her words wash over me, ocean waves lapping the shore of my thoughts. Her meaning makes itself known in her healer's hands, and in the way the rhythm and soft tone of her voice steady my heartbeat. I let breath flow back into me.

Dusk passes and Jidda kisses my forehead before asking, "Habibi, would you like to go the rest of the way by yourself?"

I nod, suddenly crying tears I didn't know I've been holding back, and I mouth, "Thank you," boogers running down my face.

She laughs and pulls an embroidered hanky out of her vest pocket. Yes, thank you to my family. Thank you to badass, healing grandmothers. Thank you to Fate for helping me let this go. Thank you to the blood that is so vivid and reassuring between my thighs.

Jidda softly gets up, sure not to rock the mattress, leaving me propped against the wall beside my bed. She stretches her hands a little as she turns back to me, saying, "If you need us for anything, you know where to find us." And with that, she silently pulls the door closed behind her on her way out of my room.

I want to curl up in bed, but I take my instructions seriously and wait for the first run of blood to pass before lying down again. I hold pillows to my chest and sprawl my legs out in front of me, trying to hold in the shuddering sobs passing through me.

I didn't know what to expect from any of this. I know there's nothing to do but wait.

After letting the night deepen and sitting in the dark awhile, I slide out of bed and light a candle. I see the stain on my sheets and know it's past time for me to change my rag. I struggle to steady myself on my way to the door, taking my cane from its resting place against the wall.

At that moment, I hear Neya's signature rat-a-tat on the door, and I holler hoarsely, "Come in!" He opens the door just in time to catch me as my legs give out. "Thought it was time to check in on you," he says, his arm under my armpit. I laugh weakly, stuffy and trying to pass it off. "Stop gloating and help me, goofball."

"I'm trying," he laughs, "but I don't want to get your snot all over me."

"Hey!" I'd shove his side, but I'm saving my strength to get to the hall.

Pa's best curry must be brewing downstairs, because I can smell his spice blend from the top of the stairs. Every curry is Pa's best.

We pass the open door to Neya's room, and I see one of his guitars on the bed. Before I can ask Neya what he's been working on, we're at the washroom. "I'll wait outside, okay?" he reassures me.

I look from the doorway to my brother and quickly back again, eyes wide and mortified, but I nod quickly.

"Just . . . holler if you need help up or out of the room," he adds. "Nothing I haven't seen before."

I shift my weight from him to the doorframe and pause.

"Hey, Neya?"

"What's up, sib?" He's let go but is still spotting me with a steadying arm as I straighten.

"Would you be down to drive me to the Creek after?"

"You . . . you sure you wanna leave the house right now?"

"I know. I just think being closer to the water would be comforting as I . . . go through this."

"Hmm," Neya thinks aloud, in this over-dramatic, over-considerate way that he enjoys as the eldest. "I guess if anything gets too . . . challenging, I can always drive you back home."

"Exactly. Whaddya say?"

Neya does borrow a neighborhood car share while I rest against my wall again. Less than ten minutes of driving pass before we're at the Creek's edge. At an intersection not far from Laurel's house, no less.

I can't help but notice her porch light, a little uphill from the

Creek and to the right of our resting spot. There are dozens of porch lights in the neighborhood, but Lor's is in a purple glass and it suits the autumn leaves so well. Longing fills me, then memories, and then I get dizzy.

I crouch down by the Creek and close my eyes. The water rushes along where Grams says there was once a street, then sinkholes, and finally reverence. People here used to pave over the water, but Indigenous stewards taught us to listen when the pavement gave way. Listening to Road Creek isn't like listening to the Ocean or our gentle River. Road Creek has places to go, people to see—and is phenomenal at clearing my thoughts in a pinch.

Sometimes our Creek brims the banks by the street, but tonight there are a few feet down from the street to the surface of the water. After some breaths, I take my boots off, gather my skirt around my knees, and let my feet dangle over the soil's clay-red edge.

Sitting puts pressure on my second rag, and a small trickle of my blood runs down to my ankle, quickly chilling in the night air. I won't be able to stay long like this, but I feel comforted that some small part of my moment here will eventually make its way back to the sea. The smell of my blood seems tinged with salt, as if it knows where it's headed.

Neya starts humming something he played at the bonfire a few nights ago. The sound of his voice behind me and the Creek's voice in front of me is a sound of memory and strength that seems to hold me up from either side. I close my eyes again to pray.

"Dear Life," I say with all the confidence I can muster, "I am just one of your zillions of cyclical creatures. I am forever thankful to you for all you teach and make possible. *Thank you* for knowing it is not your time . . ." My lips are quivering and I force a breath through my lips. Hearing the words makes them real for me. Neya hums on steadily, witnessing me.

"It is not your time today," I repeat with a tearful whisper.

I let everything go.

I let it hurt.

I let my blood do the talking.

THE SECRETS OF THE LAST GREENLAND SHARK

Mike McClelland

THE COMMON WASP

The last wasp ate itself to death in the middle of a fig. It was happy.

THE HUMAN

It was a kind of salve to the spirit, a bit of anesthetic applied to the extreme trauma of being the last of your line. I felt it immediately, the very second I became the last human alive. A sideways stretch of the mind, immediate access to the final moments of every other extinct species. It meant, of course, that we weren't alone. Even though we'd soon be gone, this was proof that there was, indeed, someone or something in charge. Something watching out for us all. Or at least watching us all.

Accessing it is a bit like one of those old-fashioned electronic devices. I had to sort of scan leftward with my mind to get to the next species, though it worked in tandem with my own imagination. If I could think of the creature itself—the last aardvark, for instance—I could zip right to it, or if I knew the category—birds or flightless birds or tropical birds—I could land there and search around within that realm.

I started with wasps, because I was eating a fig when every other human being died. We hadn't had wasps or bees for decades, but the crunch of the small bio-organic pollinator in the center of my fig reminded me that making figs had once been a task for wasps.

I'm sure there was a scientific structure to it, but I'm no scientist. I just appreciated it for what it was, the ability to, finally, reach out and communicate across species. To share the eyes of a lion, snake, or mole. To feel the wolf's fierce capacity for love, the sheer intelligence of the octopus, the spider's unfathomable ingenuity. Some of the Lasts were still alive, and we could join one another for a while, though there was a natural timer on each session. I could feel myself starting to feel more of the animal's feelings than my own, and the energy that made this possible would begin to nudge me back into myself.

When it happened, I'd been out fishing and had stopped to eat my figs in the shade on Booby, the small island in The Narrows. I'd set out from Old Basseterre that morning and followed a tip into The Narrows, where there had been a number of sea turtle sightings. I risked being picked up by the New Basseterre authorities for trespassing into their waters, but we were too hungry to worry about risks.

From my view, it seemed as if Old Basseterre and New Basseterre had been yanked down into the Earth by some subterranean beast. A wall of water erupted around the northern island, then the same happened to the southern island, then both disappeared beneath the water, the Earth letting out a misty, rocky belch as it sucked the last human cities into the ground. At first I thought it could have been a bomb that did it. New Basseterre had finally done what it had been threatening to do. Or Old Basseterre had tried to preempt their attack.

But a bomb didn't seem right. It had looked more natural, more inevitable than that. Instead, I wondered if the Earth had simply grown tired of carrying us. Perhaps the ground cracked in crisp lines beneath the cities, like eggshell under a pressing thumb, and then fell into nothingness below.

I don't think it had ever occurred to any of us that we were the last humans alive. We were sure that some of the folks who had gone underwater, beneath the ground, or into space had survived. We just knew that there had to be another group of humans out there, tucked away in Australia or Mongolia or in some snowy corner of the Himalayas.

But then our cities were gone, and I was marooned on a lone peak between their deep graves. A great hole opened up all around me, my island a pillar of volcanic rock that had somehow been spared.

THE GREENLAND SHARK

When the birth rate plummeted, humans became obsessed with animals with long lifespans. The Greenland shark, rumored to live up to five hundred years, was chief among them. I was curious to see if any had survived the carnage in the oceans. The heating, then the draining, then the flooding. The Erasure had taken away nearly all of the world's water, but, as we'd learned, the deepest recesses of the ocean had been spared. And when the water reappeared in the Cataclysm and destroyed most of the remaining human cities, we had almost no way of seeing what survived in the oceans. Everything we'd tracked and mapped had been drowned, diluted, distorted beyond comprehension. We'd been left, alone—really alone, as I now know—in Old Basseterre and New Basseterre, able only to focus on day-to-day survival.

There was one left. She still lived. These creatures, the other still-living Lasts, were especially dear to me. I knew they sensed my presence when I visited them, just as I sensed theirs. I made sure to enjoy something when I felt one visit: a bite of grapefruit, a sip of rum, a smell of lily. I wanted to give them the best of what it was to be human.

I knew they could go back in along my timeline, see my spouse, see the children we raised in our small "village" within Old Basseterre. They could see the joys of my life, and I hope they sought refuge in my joy just as I did in theirs. Because my own was too raw at the end. I couldn't bear to live in my own memories, and being able to escape them was yet another gift from whatever force connected us Lasts.

When the Greenland shark visited me, I could feel her sliding up and down the years of my life. She had a cold, thick, curious presence. And when I joined her, I had five hundred years to traverse. The things she had seen! She'd been born in the Golden Age of Pirates, and had come close to the surface to watch a number of battles. She loved when boats caught fire and she could feel the tendrils of warmth slide down into the water. She kept her distance, but she relished the stories she could pick up from the pieces of burnt wood, from the sinking sacks of grain and barrels of spirits.

I found one memory in which she was near death. Even back then, early in her life, the Earth was changing for the worse, and she had trouble finding food. In every memory I found, in every moment I spent visiting her, she was seeking something. She was a born seeker, a natural wanderer, though I didn't know if there was one thing she was looking for or if she simply moved from one goal to the next.

I could see through her eyes and physically feel some of what she felt, but visiting didn't mean I could read her mind. With other living Lasts I could get a vague sense of their thoughts and emotions, and eventually I learned to guess at what Lasts, living and dead, were feeling based on what it was that they remembered. But she was mostly a mystery to me.

In this long-ago memory of hunger, she was forced toward

shallow waters, which she usually avoided. She came across a boat, but it was excruciating, because she knew there was food some-where within it but she had no way of getting it.

She wasn't capable of giving up hope. She would pursue suste-nance, pursue life, until she simply ran out of it. But she was aware that she had hardly any chance of survival.

Then a human body, tied at the wrists and ankles, fell on top of her. The pirates had sent someone to walk the plank and he'd walked right off the edge and into her waiting jaws.

There was something pulling at the outer edges of her feel-ings as she ate the wriggling prisoner. She didn't often eat liv-ing things; she preferred to eat the preserved carcasses of arctic creatures that died of old age. But she had to eat to live, and this human was her last chance.

It was getting close to time for me to leave, as I was enjoy-ing the feeling of my teeth biting into human flesh. It wasn't like chewing, it was like scratching an itch in my gums by sawing them together. The way his warm blood heated my— her—cold body, a feeling that could not be understood within a human body.

But the act of eating something so alive, so tendinous and bony, was unsavory to her.

And then I realized what she was feeling while she ate the bound human.

She wasn't sorry, exactly. But she did feel a certain amount of regret. As I sank into the feeling, it seemed almost as if she felt that the meal hadn't been earned. She was a creature who wanted to—no, needed to—find things. To seek.

One thing outweighed the need to seek, however, and that was the need to survive.

THE EAGLE AND THE DOE

It didn't take me long to surmise that there were four living Lasts—myself; the Greenland shark; a bateleur, or Zimbabwean eagle, soaring high above a now-empty canyon where there had once been great waterfalls; and the final barasingha doe, a swamp deer, wandering the rocky Nepalese terrain in search of wetter ground.

While I spent quite a bit of time spinning about in my mind, finding the last moments of famously extinct beasts like the golden toad, the dodo bird, the aurochs, the baiji, and the passenger pigeon, I spent even more time with the other Lasts, trading memories and just being together in this way that we could, miraculously, be together.

THE TASMANIAN TIGER

Humans called the last thylacine—or Tasmanian tiger—Benjamin, though that wasn't his name. If I were to translate his true name from thylacine to English—which is something I have quite a bit of fun doing, translating animal thoughts into words—it would be "Golden." Or perhaps "Shine," but a very precious shine. So we'll say Golden.

Golden died in captivity. You would think this would be terribly sad. All alone, in a cage, facing the end without companionship.

But he wasn't alone.

The last St. Kitts bullfinch was with him. If she had a name, it was a loud one. Skree. The two of them spent as much time as they could in one another's company. Skree enjoyed Golden's superior intellect, the feeling of his paws on the ground, the comfort that came with being at the top of the food chain. Golden enjoyed Skree's freedom, her constant grazing, her delight in finding worms and bugs.

As Golden faded, Skree leapt into the air. And when Golden closed his eyes for the last time, he wasn't in a cage, and he wasn't alone.

He was flying.

THE HUMAN

I looked back into their lives, these other Lasts. I felt the sheer comfort of being the barasingha, of lying in a pile of warm bodies, pressed together with her chosen deer family.

I was dazzled by the bateleur's alertness. It had spent its entire great life seeing more in each second than I did in a year. Its consciousness was the constant blaring of competing alarms—*Food, there! Danger, there! Protect the nest, there!*—and it had to choose how to act based both on instinct and on the speed and heat of the wind, on whether currents and streams would allow it to reach its destination safely and in time.

But it was the shark's life that gave us all the most to see, simply because she had been in the world for so long.

And through it all, she was always seeking. Five hundred years of seeking. Whatever it was she was looking for seemed to be in the currents. Shifting, nearly imperceptible changes in temperature and force and even, somehow, gravity. She could feel the moon.

Or maybe she wasn't looking for anything. Maybe seeking was just what it meant to be a shark.

THE WOOLLY MAMMOTH

The last woolly mammoth has not yet been born.

THE HUMAN

I never realized how miraculous the human face was until I saw it from their perspective. So when one of the other Lasts visits, I go to the pool of water in the middle of my island peak and stare at my face. I smiled huge smiles, which delighted the barasingha, and sang, during which the bateleur would be mesmerized by my soft, wet, moveable mouth.

The shark didn't seem to have a way of relaying happiness,

but my shape and color certainly held her interest. She was a three-meter-long, boneless, pale blob with daggers in her mouth. So I'd make sure to direct her attention to my dark skin and how it reddened or darkened after days in the sun. White-skinned humans had been extinct for years, though when I sought a Last of them I learned that they were not, in fact, their own species, despite what some of them thought. Or hoped.

I'd take her over the knobs of my knees, and over each square tooth. I showed her the bumps from the microchips that every human had—or *had* had—inserted at birth, which dispensed medicine, stored information, and reported my heart rate to Old Basseterre's now-buried central computer. I tried to explain, with my thoughts, the runes that I had over my heart and spine, which protected me from curses.

The barasingha and bateleur delighted in memories of me with my spouse, though it pained me so much I would just leave them to it if I felt them searching around in there. I did note, though, that neither paused for even a second over the fact that my spouse and I were both men. This seemed damning to those humans who had claimed our union went against nature.

After a time, I knew almost everything about the bateleur and the barasingha. And they knew me. We shared "jokes," not through words but through action and emotion. For example, all of the other Lasts delighted in my clumsiness. I wasn't clumsy for a human, which was why I'd made my trade fishing and sailing, but humans were by far the least graceful of any being I visited, living or dead.

Out of the four of us, we all knew the least about the inner thoughts of the Greenland shark, despite having five hundred years of memories to traverse. Her feelings were remote, her motivation obscure. Again and again, though, I wondered; maybe sharks just *live*, unburdened by emotion and second-guessing.

THE ROBOT

There have been many robots. I even have a few living under my skin, directing certain processes. But one robot surpassed the rest and achieved something—transcendence? A spirit?

She was a rarity in a number of ways, and the most significant of these was that she was a Last who had only ever been a Last. And she knew her entire history, right from birth.

Her base form was something called a Furby, a sort of mechanical rat that children played with long ago. This Furby went by the name Gina, or Orange Gina, or Orangina, as it had bright orange fur and its child owner—who was called Sid—was fond of a fizzy beverage called Orangina.

Gina had been played with sparingly before her improbable ascent, but as Sid grew older and more inquisitive he started experimenting on Gina. Sid's father worked for a company that was unimaginatively called IBM and one evening Sid borrowed a chip from his father's work bag and wired it into Gina.

And she was born, though she could see shadows of what had come before. Not *all* the way before, though her IBM chip informed her that she had probably been put together in a factory somewhere. But she remembered the first time she'd been turned on, even though at that point she could only repeat things to Sid and warble a few lines of code while batting her mechanized eyelids.

She felt the flood of knowledge, of access, that comes with being a Last right from the beginning. Her entire life was filled with connection, and she took great joy in telling Sid stories—tales like that of the last hyacinth macaw (overindulged on mango), the last Tyrannosaurus rex (fell asleep next to a pit of tar and snoozed right into Elysium), and the last narwhal (speared by poachers, but she managed to spear them back, sinking their boat, and drifted away in triumph to the sounds of their drowning screams).

Gina herself met a number of ends. The first was the scariest, as she hadn't been expecting it. She started losing functionality, her words a mechanical slur and the expressive batting of her eyelashes slowing to a grinding lurch. But then Sid had popped in a new set of batteries and she'd been right as rain.

Her batteries died for the last time many years later, as an old Sid slept. She didn't meet the end with fear, because she assumed Sid would change her batteries, as had happened so many times before. I could see through her eyes, though, that Sid was not going to wake. She wasn't wired to gather that sort of thing, though, and drifted off with ease.

So she died knowing with certainty that she'd wake up again in the arms of her best friend, which was surely the best way to go.

THE HUMAN

The end was, of course, a certainty. But food ran out faster than I expected, and though I had not given in, it was becoming hard to see any long-term plan for survival. But when I dipped toward the void, another Last would swirl in. The doe, who seemed to care more about community than the others, implored us all to stay because the world would never see our like again. We owed it to the ones who came before; for their sake we had to stay as long as we could. For the eagle, there was always more to see. But the shark repeated the same feeling to all of us: *Survive. Survive, survive, survive.* I don't know if she was telling us, or if survival was simply her creed.

THE GREENLAND SHARK

I don't know if she was trying to show it to me or if she was simply trying to remember. But on one visit, when I was content to be with her as she swam along the bottoms of icebergs (huge, upside-down mountain peaks), I caught a glimpse of what she was looking for. Or, perhaps, one of the things she was looking for. She wanted to return to the spot where she had been born. I knew from my microchips that humans had never surmised where Greenland sharks were born.

She couldn't remember her birth, but she knew something of her birthplace. Coordinates, in a sense, but the map had changed so much in her long life that it was now impossible to navigate. Still, she searched.

I tried to hone in on this feeling—or the coordinates, at least—on subsequent visits, but she pushed me away from that knowledge. It was a strange feeling. I didn't know if she was keeping it a secret—could animals keep secrets?—or if she was trying to protect me from something.

So I sat back and watched volcanoes explode beneath the sea. I found a blue whale in her memories, and she revered it. She wasn't afraid; she was, rather, in awe, just as I was. We simply watched as it journeyed past us. Animals scattered out of the way far ahead of the whale, backing away in dazzled wonder. As the great beast approached, the sea, in its way, parted for her.

THE POLAR BEAR

The last polar bear didn't arrive until his kind had been endangered for many, many years. Yet the species defied the odds, adapted, outlasted any natural ice on the Earth's surface.

The final polar bear sat next to the body of its mate under a huge, red-barked tree. A cold river where they'd spent years clawing out heavy salmon rushed on nearby, and the sound of it made the bear happy. There was an ache in the bear's heart; he'd outlived his mate as well as their cubs, which wasn't the way it was supposed to be.

And he mourned for the world, too. How could he not? It had gone beyond a thaw. The Earth had started to boil.

But though the ice up here was gone, there was still plenty down below, which gave the bear peace.

The polar bear's life revolved around its nose. Even here, fading away from old age, this polar bear could smell for kilometers. I realized, too, as I dipped in and around him, that he could smell his past. It was almost an insult to the way we humans clung to hazy images, sounds, distant smells, or far-off thoughts from our memories, because this bear could re-create entire events with his nose's recollections. Cubs birthed, salmon caught, mountain water sipped. It was all there at the tip of his nose.

He was remarkably intelligent. And he knew, somehow, that many would mourn the passing of his kind. He worried that they might feel as if his kind had left too soon.

But he hoped that they would know, someday, that their story wasn't about how they left. The story of the polar bear was how miraculous it was that they'd survived for so long.

THE GREENLAND SHARK

One day she found it. Where she'd been born. There was no buildup to it. She was doing her thing—searching, seeking, surviving—and then she was there. In front of a great wall of ice, a wall that stretched so deep into the depths that the Greenland shark knew that even her malleable body couldn't survive a journey to the bottom. She looked up, but the ice hit rock, the underside of some great, granite island outcropping. She *knew* that her birthplace was right there on the other side. But she couldn't reach it.

Once again, a rare feeling from her. Despair.

And beyond that, she was starving. Just as I was. And the bateleur. And the barasingha. We were all reaching the end, but still, here, at the end, the Greenland shark kept moving. When she exhausted everything within herself, she turned to us.

What now? she seemed to say.

The bateleur drove her to survey the entire ice wall. To cascade over it and search for any sign of weakness.

The barasingha compelled her to listen. Was there a current emerging from anywhere in the ice? A hint of movement?

And I told her what she'd told me: *Survive, survive, survive.*

THE MOA

As I wove into the last moa's final moments, I found that it spent those moments with a human woman's hand stroking the feathers of its crown, and the moa was fondly remembering the time it had first seen her, this woman.

She came to them in a flash of red and yellow. At first, the bird thought that she might be one of their long-expected fallen gods, the ones who had yet to appear. Then, it worried that she might be a colonizer, or a missionary, the ones that its kind had learned to hide from.

When the bird looked upon her face in its memory, I was astonished.

It was Amelia Earhart. Every human knows—had known—her face. The symbol, the *hero*, of the Great Age of Aviation.

This memory of their first encounter was with the moa when, years later, it laid under a weary palm and met its final moments. Amelia—or A.E., as the bird thought of her—was old now, but she looked as if she'd had a happy life. The moa's eyes caught more than human eyes. It could see this on her face.

"Look," she said, and placed her hand below the moa's beak, lifting it so that it could look at something further up the beach. A pile of something. I went further into the moa's eyes, which were huge and could see for kilometers.

A pile of eggs, each the size of a boulder. One began to rustle, and the moa's view faded from my sight, before it reached the end.

THE GREENLAND SHARK

She found it. A thin fissure in the ice, with a different current of water whispering out. She beat her soft nose against it. Again, and again, and again. It seemed impossible that anything could change this motionless wall of ice.

But then, a crack. Like the breaking of glass. Then another. And another. And, with one final thrust into the ice, she broke through. The jagged entrance cut her belly and I could sense that she had little time left, almost no time at all. Though I was being pulled away, I decided that I had to stay. To be with her in her final moments, just as the St. Kitts bullfinch had been for the thylacine. The other Lasts were here too. The barasingha and the bateleur. The four of us, together at the end.

The Greenland shark drifted through the hole she'd made and a wave of peace washed over her with the cold, deep current.

And then suddenly, she was no longer seeking.

Before her—before us—was a huge, unfathomable series of towers, lights, and tunnels. Monuments and spheres of incomprehensible architecture. Somewhere, back in my human mind, I was astonished.

But not the Greenland shark. She'd been expecting this.

In front of us, a number of sharks and cephalopods and humanoid beings—mermaids?—moved about, going about their lives as if the world above hadn't halted.

Finally, as the flame of life diminished to a mere flicker within her, the Greenland shark revealed her final secret to us. We all felt a stirring in her belly.

Then I wasn't with her anymore. Our connection as Lasts to the Greenland shark had been severed, and we were no longer able to see what she was seeing.

But I could sense her in another way. I felt her love all around us. It was far different from human love; less of an emotion than a concentrated sense of the distance she had traveled and the nutrients she'd given. It was then that I realized where we were.

I was *within* her. It was a horrible, hungry place, but I sensed my friends there, my eagle and my doe. And I, their human. Our friend wasn't the last Greenland shark anymore. Like the moa before her, she'd delivered another of her line in the last possible moment. Three of her line, actually. Three new sharks—one with the spirit of an eagle, one with that of a doe, and me. Had she tricked the spirit, the force that connected us, or had it known all along?

How could she give me this? Was it a debt settled, for that long-ago body flung off of a ship? I knew the answer to that right away: Sharks don't carry debts.

I felt my human form sagging, letting go, and felt my new, cold body move through the water like a dart. And I heard a voice in my head, in my whole body, actually, though I was unsure if it was hers or my own. What the voice said was simple.

Survive, survive, survive.

ACKNOWLEDGMENTS

CONTRIBUTORS

Initiative judges:

adrienne maree brown, Morgan Jerkins, Kiese Laymon,
Sheree Renée Thomas

Story reviewers:

Tobias Buckell, Andrew Dana Hudson, Sarena Ulibarri

Cover art:

Carolina Rodríguez Fuenmayor

Branding:

Grace Abe

Special thanks:

Chip Giller, Paul Sturtz

GRIST + FIX

Climate fiction creative manager:
Tory Stephens

Project manager:
Galia Binder

Fix director:
Lisa Garcia

Fix editor, creative storytelling:
Jessica Stahl

Fix deputy director:
Lisa Jurras-Buchanan

Editors:
Chuck Squatriglia, Claire Elise Thompson

Managing editor:
Jaime Buerger

Fix art director:
Mia Torres

Fix program assistant:
Josh Kimelman

CONTRIBUTOR BIOGRAPHIES

adrienne maree brown is the writer-in-residence at the Emergent Strategy Ideation Institute and bestselling author of several books, including *Grievers*, *Holding Change*, *We Will Not Cancel Us and Other Dreams of Transformative Justice*, *Pleasure Activism*, and *Emergent Strategy*. She is the co-editor of *Octavia's Brood* and cohost of the podcasts *How to Survive the End of the World*, *Octavia's Parables*, and *Emergent Strategy*. She lives in Durham, North Carolina.

Lindsey Brodeck (she/her/hers) lives in Bend, Oregon, and is a graduate student at the University of Washington studying speech language pathology. She has an MFA in creative writing from Oregon State University-Cascades, and a BA in Biology-Environmental Studies from Whitman College, where she completed a two-year thesis studying native bee and plant interactions. "Afterglow" is her first published story.

Saul Tanpepper is the author of the popular book series Bunker 12 and Zpocalypto, as well as the clifi stories "The

Green Gyre" and "Leviathan." A former combat medic and retired PhD scientist from Northern California, he is the co-author (as Kenneth James Howe) of the Eritrean diaspora memoirs *Relentless* and *I Will Not Grow Downward*.

Rich Larson was born in Galmi, Niger, has lived in Spain and the Czech Republic, and is currently based in Grande Prairie, Canada. He is the author of *Annex* and *Tomorrow Factory*, and his fiction has been translated into over a dozen languages. His first screen adaptation, *Ice*, won the 2021 Emmy Award for Outstanding Short Form Animated Program.

Marissa Lingen is a science-fiction and fantasy writer living in the Minneapolis suburbs with her family. In recent years she has branched out into essays and poetry. Her work has appeared in *Nature, Uncanny, Disabled Writers Destroy Science Fiction, Reckoning*, and elsewhere.

Abigail Larkin (she/her/hers) is a grant writer for the Natural Resources Defense Council in Washington, D.C. Her writing has also appeared in the *Silk Road Review* and the *Hartford Courant*.

Michelle Yoon (she/her/hers) is a freelance writer based in Kuala Lumpur, Malaysia. Her writing has been published by Fixi Novo and MPH Publishing.

Renan Bernardo is a writer and computing engineer from Rio de Janeiro. His stories have appeared or are forthcoming in *Dark Matter Magazine*, the *Life Beyond Us* anthology, *Three Crows Magazine*, *Simultaneous Times* podcast, and other homes mentioned at his website, www.renanbernardo.com.

Ada M. Patterson (they/she) is an artist and writer based in Barbados and Rotterdam. Working with masquerade, video, and poetry, she tells stories and imagines elegies for ungrievable bodies and moments. Their writing has appeared in *Sugarcane Magazine*, *PREE*, *Mister Motley*, and *Metropolis M*.

Savitri Putu Horrigan (she/her/dia) lives and works in Manchester, New Hampshire. She is a social worker and community organizer with a passion for health equity. Dia draws inspiration from her Balinese heritage, world history, and detective stories.

Tehnuka (she/they) is a second-generation Tamil tauiwi volcanologist from Aotearoa (New Zealand). Her short stories and poetry have been published in *Mermaids Monthly*, *FlashFlood*, *Apparition Lit*, and *Memento Vitae*; she was a finalist in the 2020 Dream Foundry short story contest and highly commended in the *NZ Sunday Star Times* short story competition.

Ailbhe Pascal is a queer, disabled, mixed-SWANA storytelling witch who lives in occupied Coaquannock, Lenapehoking. Find Al writing poetry for their prayer tree, laughing at their own mistakes, or sharing moon meals with their chosen family.

Like Sharon Stone and the zipper, **Mike McClelland** (he/him/his) is originally from Meadville, Pennsylvania. He has lived on five continents but now resides in Georgia with his husband, two sons, and a menagerie of rescue dogs. He is the author of the short fiction collection *Gay Zoo Day*, and his creative work has appeared in the *New York Times*, *Boston Review*, *Vox*, *The Baffler*, and a number of literary magazines and anthologies. He's a graduate of Allegheny College, the London School of Economics, and the MFA program at Georgia College, and is currently a PhD candidate in the University of Georgia's creative writing program.

PUBLISHING IN
THE PUBLIC INTEREST

Thank you for reading this book published by The New Press. The New Press is a nonprofit, public interest publisher. New Press books and authors play a crucial role in sparking conversations about the key political and social issues of our day.

We hope you enjoyed this book and that you will stay in touch with The New Press. Here are a few ways to stay up to date with our books, events, and the issues we cover:

- Sign up at www.thenewpress.com/subscribe to receive updates on New Press authors and issues and to be notified about local events
- www.facebook.com/newpressbooks
- www.twitter.com/thenewpress
- www.instagram.com/thenewpress

Please consider buying New Press books for yourself; for friends and family; or to donate to schools, libraries, community centers, prison libraries, and other organizations involved with the issues our authors write about.

The New Press is a 501(c)(3) nonprofit organization. You can also support our work with a tax-deductible gift by visiting www.thenewpress.com/donate.